Crackmammoth

GARY LEE VINCENT

Burning Bulb
PUBLISHING

Crackmammoth
By **Gary Lee Vincent**

Burning Bulb Publishing
P.O. Box 4721
Bridgeport, WV 26330-4721
United States of America
www.BurningBulbPublishing.com

Cover designed by Max Cave as a work for hire for Gary Lee Vincent and Burning Bulb Publishing.

First Edition.

Paperback Edition ISBN: 978-1-964172-22-4

Also by Gary Lee Vincent

Novels
PASSAGEWAY
BELLY TIMBER
ATTACK OF THE MELONHEADS
WHEN THE BEDPOSTS SHAKE (RING OF THE SUCCUBUS)
IMPOUND
STRANGE FRIENDS
THE BEST ACTORS THAT EVER LIVED
JEROME
THE BLIND MELODY

Darkened—The West Virginia Vampire Series
DARKENED HILLS
DARKENED HOLLOWS
DARKENED WATERS
DARKENED SOULS
DARKENED MINDS
DARKENED DESTINIES

The Douglas River Vampire Series
RIVER: A VAMPIRE'S NIGHTMARE
ICARUS

Dedicated to
Anyone who has read the series up to this far.
Thank you.

CHAPTER 1

Tucked away in the West Virginian countryside, the Futures Bioresearch facility (F-Bio for short) wasn't really the kind of place to attract undue attention from the public.

When asked what the institute's business was, Dr. Milton Ambrose always replied, "Oh, we handle contracts for medical and pharmaceutical companies. Drug-related research and stuff like that."

That, of course, was the official line, and was actually what F-Bio had initially gone into business to do. But, one way or another, as luck (or fate) would have it, F-Bio had ended up working closely with the US Government on completely different areas of scientific research.

The national and state governments (and, to a lesser degree, the West Virginian police) had suddenly realized the benefits of having such a secluded facility in such an out-of-the-way location. It meant they could drop off bothersome or cutting-edge projects there.

Or projects they don't want the public hearing about yet, Milton Ambrose thought to himself with a grim smile. *Projects like Snuffy, for instance.*

On this particular day, a Saturday, Dr. Ambrose was working in Lab 7, the last laboratory in the smaller of the two buildings that formed the L-shaped Futures Bioresearch facility. Now, he looked up from the research papers he was studying and smiled.

We're so secluded here—well out in the West Virginian mountains, with just the Sleepaway Campground and Lake Placid and its trailer park nearby—that we could be working out how to destroy the human race entirely and no one would cotton on until it was way too late to avert disaster.

Feeling like he needed to stretch his legs, Dr. Ambrose got up to his feet and walked over to look out through one of the windows on the north wall of the laboratory. From here, he could see the high wire fence that ringed the building, a precaution against hungry bears, lost campers, and nosy folks from the trailer park.

It was early October now, with autumn well in season, and most of the trees around the facility had shed at least half of their leaves. Oddly enough, because the woods were so thick around here, this partial denuding of their covering hardly increased visibility into the forest depths. At least not from where Dr. Ambrose stood.

The late evening lighting revealed a sort of spectacle of nature

As Milton Ambrose watched, a powerful wind blew a swirling brown, golden, and red confetti of leaves through the air and deposited them in a pile against the wall of the long silver extension to Lab 7 that F-Bio had recently built.

The laboratory extension was shaped like a giant Quonset hut, and Dr. Ambrose watched another airborne stream of autumn leaves blow against it and drip down its sides.

As if in sympathy with the weather, 'Snuffy' trumpeted loudly.

Dr. Ambrose grinned at the sound the animal made. It was a peculiar sound, one that hadn't been heard on Earth for about 4,000 years.

And I'm the custodian of the creature making it, he thought with delight, staring across the laboratory at the door that granted access into Snuffy's quarters.

At that moment, Dr. Milton Ambrose felt on top of the world.

CHAPTER 2

Milton Ambrose was sixty years old. He was of both middle height and weight, white-haired and balding.

Dr. Ambrose had been married once but had thrown himself fully into his work since his divorce over twenty years ago. This reaction had been partly to escape the pain of his marriage's breakup, and partly to avoid the problems of beginning and navigating a fresh relationship.

He was pretty good-looking and still had no shortage of female admirers amongst those he worked with. Still, aside from the occasional romantic dalliance, he mainly avoided work-related contact with the fair sex.

Milton Ambrose's hard work had paid off. Now, at age sixty, he was one of America's leading researchers on induced pluripotent stem cells, the foundation for bringing the Woolly Mammoth back from extinction. Here at F-Bio, Milton Ambrose was one of their most respected scientists, with a lot of authority.

Two months ago, while excavating a spot for a new Marcellus Shale mining operation in nearby Randolph County, the workers had discovered the body of a young and completely preserved male woolly mammoth. Like a giant bug, the mammoth was encased in amber.

After cutting the mammoth out of the ground but leaving its amber casing intact, the workers left the animal standing while they decided what to do with it.

One phone call led to another, and in a few days, the animal had been deposited in Milton Ambrose's care at F-Bio.

This wasn't accidental. One of the most clandestine—i.e., 'tell you and kill you'—projects currently going on in the Futures Bioresearch labs had to do with the reanimation of dead organic tissue.

And somewhere along the bureaucratic paper trail involved in dealing with the unearthed mammoth corpse, someone had made a joke about seeing if Ambrose's crazy ideas really worked.

He'd reported success with bringing cockroaches back to life for a few minutes, so they'd decided to give him a *real* challenge.

And so, Ambrose got the 'fossil.'

CHAPTER 3

It had been a day just like any other when they'd begun the process of reanimating the mammoth.

Except for the dense brown fur coat that covered his body, the creature lying on his side on the laboratory table in Lab 7 could have been a baby elephant and not something from the prehistoric Ice Age.

Seen from the rear (with his head out of view), Dr. Ambrose even thought the animal could be mistaken for a small bear.

The animal's hide was pierced by tubes that carried a dark mixture of synthetic blood and the project's secret reanimating fluids back and forth from his body to the pump that did the work of his heart until it came alive again—if it did. The pump had been working non-stop for four hours now, and by now, the reanimation fluid was certain to have saturated the young mammoth's body tissue.

Monitors were clamped to shaven areas of the animal's body to keep track of his vital signs. At the moment, he had none, still being very dead. After being freed from his amber overcoat, the mammoth had been kept in the laboratory's largest freezer.

This morning, he had been thawed out, and now . . .

And now we'll see if my damn calculations were correct or not, Dr. Ambrose had thought to himself while subconsciously gesturing to the two thick cables that had been implanted right at the base of the mammoth's tusks.

He'd almost found himself laughing at the sight of him and his five colleagues, the expectant looks on their faces; the mingling of surface excitement and underlying apprehension.

Positioned on tripods around the room, with one of them directly overhead, four video cameras had filmed this historic event.

This whole scenario makes me feel like we're mad scientists in a Frankenstein flick. Waking the Frankenstein monster up proved to be a disaster for everyone. What if this ends up the same way?

"What was that, Doc?" one of the assisting scientists had asked him.

"Huh?" Milton Ambrose had had no idea that he'd spoken aloud. "Oh, nothing," he'd added after getting control of his thoughts again. "I'm just hoping we've properly gauged the amount of electric power we need to apply—too much and we'll fry the animal; too little, and we may—to borrow a phrase—not 'power him up' sufficiently."

The scientists had laughed at that.

Milton Ambrose had inspected that all connections to the mammoth were as they should be and had then gestured across the room to Paula Helmsworth, the female assistant standing beside the potentiometers and a barrel of conductive fluid that reminded Milton of the Trixon barrel from *Return of the Living Dead.* He stifled a grin.

"Okay, time to see how smart we all are," he had told the young woman. "Feed our hairy elephant with electric juice, Paula."

Paula hit the power switch, and the instrument dials instantly leaped to full. An audible humming sound filled the laboratory as the electric connection between the machine and the mammoth was made.

Dr. Ambrose had thought he smelled meat frying somewhere, most probably in his mind.

The dead beast shook on the table as electricity surged through him.

As programmed into the electrical equipment, the current cut out after ten seconds.

"Monitors?" Dr. Ambrose had asked one of the male technicians.

The man had shaken his head. "Nothing yet, but I did observe the barest flicker of movement. So, I think two more times might do it."

Dr. Milton Ambrose had nodded to Paula. "Again. This time, up the voltage by fifty percent."

"Do you wanna cook him for lunch?" Paula had asked. "Because I could've sworn I smelled meat frying just now."

Most of the scientists had laughed at that.

Dr. Ambrose had sighed. He glanced over at one of the four video cameras recording this resurrection attempt and shook his head.

Paula really has no sense of gravity. I can't imagine what would happen if her words got out in public.

"Point taken," he'd agreed after some reflection. "Still, up it by fifty percent, but reduce the time we shock the animal to six seconds."

Next, he'd said, by way of explanation, "Each time we shock him without wakening him, we're liable to be damaging his tissues, meaning we're reducing our chances of success. So, we need to go for broke here. Either this second attempt will awaken this creature, or we'll be back to experimenting on roaches and mice again."

Paula Helmsworth had nodded and turned the dial that increased the voltage. Once this was done, she'd nodded again at Dr. Ambrose. "Ready, sir."

"Do it."

Paula had flicked the switch again.

This time, everyone had seen the difference when electricity hit the dead animal. Afterward, they'd all found it hard to explain in words what they'd witnessed just then. Maybe there was no natural way to describe watching a dead thing come back to life.

But right before the electric current had cut out for the second time, the dead mammoth had opened his eyes, twisted his head side to side, and then let out a weak but insistent trump from his trunk.

He had kept up this sound while the five humans stared at him in shock, unable to believe they'd actually succeeded in reviving a 15,000-year-old beast.

Paula Helmsworth had been the first person to thaw from her state of awe. She'd walked over to the mammoth and grinned down at him.

"Hey, he's really cute," she'd said, stroking the animal's hairy ears. "I think we should call him 'Snuffy.'"

"Huh? Snuffy?" Dr. Ambrose asked. "Why would you want to call him that?"

Paula had laughed. "Oh, you know, Doc—Mr. Snuffleupagus on Sesame Street. Only, Snuffy here's a lot smaller."

Dr. Ambrose had smiled and nodded. "Yeah, okay, Paula. 'Snuffy' it is, then. One name is as good as any other." He'd gestured around to the other scientists who'd now crowded around the revived mammoth, which still looked dazed and confused, like he had no idea what was going.

"First of all, increase the flow to his feeding line. Now that we've got this young guy alive, we need to keep him that way."

Everyone had instantly gotten to work doing the jobs they'd rehearsed for this procedure. They'd worked with a dedication born from the knowledge of how rare an event they were all involved in.

Dr. Milton Ambrose and his staff had been very aware that if this young woolly mammoth died on them, they had zero chance of finding another one to revive.

The rest, as they say, is history.

CHAPTER 4

"Well, it *will be* history once the world gets to hear about it," Dr. Ambrose grumbled aloud to himself. "But at the moment, the top brass are shushing us. How the hell are we ever gonna earn our Nobel prizes if no one knows what we've accomplished here?"

With that grumpy thought in mind, Dr. Ambrose decided to visit Snuffy the Wooly Mammoth.

I just hope nothing happens to our living miracle of science before we can present it to the world, Milton thought as he walked towards the entrance to Snuffy's enclosure.

"Dr. Ambrose?" a female voice called behind him.

He turned to face his assistant Paula Helmsworth.

Paula Helmsworth was young and attractive. She was very competent in her work and because of this, was one of his favorite laboratory assistants.

He smiled as she approached him. "Yes, Paula?" he asked. "Do you need to see me about something?"

She shook her head. "No, sir. I was just surprised to still find you here in the lab. I thought you'd already left for home."

"Just about to, Paula, just about to," he replied. "But first, I want to check on Snuffy."

On hearing this, Paula grinned broadly. "That's what brought me up here. I was coming to feed him."

"Well, let's see him together then. I'll wait while you get out his food supplements from the safe."

He perched himself on the edge of the table that extended along the wall and watched her walk over to the safe he'd mentioned.

Almost like an idol to be worshipped, the safe stood alone on the table that had belonged to Dr. Annabelle Cole, the previous owner of this laboratory.

Dr. Cole was truly a brilliant woman, Milton Ambrose thought as an image of the woman came to his mind. *What the hell happened to her, only God knows.*

A few months ago, Annabelle Cole had come to work as usual, stayed late at work as was usual, and then very unusually, vanished.

The next morning, Annabelle Cole's car was still outside in the parking lot, while she herself was nowhere to be found. To further complicate matters, her handbag (with all of her ID documents in it) was still in the laboratory, along with her work laptop, which she took everywhere she went.

And those smears on the floor, almost like something consumed her. But what could that have been? The cops still have no idea what went on in here that night!

Paula had just gotten through entering the combination on the safe, and it clicked open.

Dr. Ambrose straightened up a little so he could look around Paula's body and see into the safe.

The safe was ordinary enough, but its contents weren't. The packages of dietary supplement for their pet mammoth were arranged on the top shelf of the safe. Miscellaneous medications were on the middle shelf, and packs of the narcotic substance named Agent Orange lay on the bottom shelf.

How many times do I need to keep repeating that it's a bad idea to store those two drugs together? Dr. Ambrose thought grimly, as Paula pulled a few large chunks of Snuffy's dietary supplements out of one of the transparent packages on the top shelf. The supplement was a bright orange in color.

Dr. Ambrose's problem was that Agent Orange—the narcotic on the bottom shelf—was also bright orange in color. Both supplement and narcotic also had a similar waxen texture.

The single visual difference between both compounds was that the food supplements came in regular-sized cubes, while the narcotic didn't.

"You seem bothered, doctor," Paula said after she'd locked the safe again and walked over to his side.

He gestured over at the safe. "I dislike narcotics. I still don't see why we have to keep that Agent Orange stuff here in our lab. What if it contaminates Snuffy's diet?"

Paula thought about this for a little while, holding her handful of orange chemical cubes up to the light.

"Ha ha, you're right, Doc. Other than that, viewed side by side, they could very well be the same thing."

"The only way to really tell them apart is to taste them," Dr. Ambrose told Paula.

She gave him a curious look. "Did you?"

He nodded. "Yes, because I wanted to be certain I could separate them if they ever got mixed up."

"What does Agent Orange taste like?" Paula enquired further.

"Like something that was never meant to be ingested by humans," was his reply. "Agent Orange has a bitter, slightly sour taste to it. Snuffy's food supplements, on the other hand are sweetly flavored to ensure that the mammoth eats them; they have to be, to mask the taste of the included antibiotics."

"Well, that's cool then," Paula said. "That should ensure they never get mixed up."

Dr. Ambrose gestured towards the entrance to Snuffy's enclosure. "There seems to be more Agent Orange in the safe than previously," he told Paula.

"There is. The state police brought some more over. They still want us to work out why the drug is so damn addictive. Dr. Huey's supposed to work on it, but he's on leave."

Dr. Ambrose nodded at that. Prior to her disappearance Dr. Cole and her assistant had made great strides in their study of Agent Orange. Dr. Cole's research notes were still here in the lab.

"Well, the sooner Huey resumes work again and takes that stuff off of our hands, the less chance of sample contamination for us," he told Paula.

As Dr. Ambrose approached Snuffy's enclosure, a sudden unease settled over him. He had spent years in pursuit of this moment—bringing back an extinct species—but the gnawing sense of danger crept into his thoughts more frequently now. What if we're not in control anymore? He stopped short, staring through the thick, reinforced glass of Snuffy's habitat. The mammoth's gentle demeanor was comforting, but the flicker of unpredictability behind its ancient eyes stirred something deep within him. They had unlocked a door to the past—who was to say that they hadn't also unleashed something far darker?

Paula's arrival broke his reverie. She handed him a set of updated vitals, her face bright but cautious. "Snuffy's responding well to the new supplement mixture," she said, forcing a smile.

Ambrose nodded but barely registered her words. His mind was elsewhere—on the rumors circulating through the higher echelons of government. The whispers of military interest, of using genetic resurrection for purposes beyond mere curiosity. He felt a cold chill. The thought of Snuffy as a weapon, manipulated into something monstrous, left him momentarily breathless. They hadn't just brought back a mammoth; they'd potentially unearthed a new kind of threat.

Before Paula could leave, Ambrose spoke, his voice quieter than usual. "We need to keep an eye on Snuffy's behavior, Paula. If you notice anything—anything out of the ordinary, no matter how small—report it immediately."

Paula furrowed her brow. "Do you think something's wrong?"

Ambrose hesitated, then shook his head. "No, nothing's wrong. But we can't be too careful. We've revived something that hasn't existed for thousands of years. There's no telling what might happen next." As she walked away, Ambrose stared again at the massive creature resting peacefully. His instincts told him that this was only the beginning—and that the storm was yet to come.

CHAPTER 5

To keep the woolly mammoth happy, Snuffy's enclosure was chilled to an artic temperature.

To work in there for any extended period of time, Dr. Ambrose and his assistants normally donned well-insulated thermal jumpsuits that made them look like they were at the North Pole.

But this was merely feeding time, so today neither the doctor nor Paula bothered to suit up.

Once through the enclosure door, however, both immediately regretted their decision.

"Damn, I keep forgetting how frigid it is in here," Milton Ambrose told Paula when the cold hit them.

"Well, I can see why the dinosaurs all died out during the Ice Age," Paula quipped and then hurried over to the food bins to roll out a pre-packed meal for Snuffy. "Even cold-blooded animals must draw the line at some point. There's cold, and then there's *cold*. The dino's blood must've frozen stiff in their veins."

Shivering visibly, Dr. Milton Ambrose walked directly to the mammoth's cage.

"Greetings, oh noble member of Mammuthus primigenius," Dr. Ambrose declaimed at the animal.

'Snuffy' was lying on his side in his cage, up near the cage's central rock formation. The cage was over fifteen feet high, ten yards deep, and five yards wide. Snuffy had more than enough space to walk around or even run if he wanted to, but the walls of the Quonset hut were reinforced so he couldn't accidentally break out or intruders accidentally break in. Along with the rock formations that simulated mountain conditions, several arctic shrubs had been planted in the animal's cage to give it a semblance of its natural habitat.

On hearing Dr. Ambrose's voice, Snuffy got up to his feet and shambled over towards him.

Dr. Ambrose nodded with delight as he watched him come on. Snuffy had a look of recognition in his eyes, like a dog got on seeing its owner. Snuffy smelt like a dog, too.

In addition, the revived animal was very intelligent and not at all belligerent. Since his revival, Snuffy had shown no signs of violence. He got along with everyone and, most importantly, he seemed to be in perfect health.

Up close, Dr. Ambrose was impressed by how large the woolly mammoth had grown in the past two months. Back when he'd arrived here, he'd been roughly the size of a calf, but now, he was already three feet taller than Dr. Ambrose, almost nine feet tall.

This increase in height bothered Dr. Ambrose somewhat. It made him worry that the food supplements they were adding to the mammoth's diet might be accelerating his growth.

But then, how the hell do we know how fast mammoths grew up back then? We're projecting Snuffy's rate of growth based on how long it takes an elephant to reach adulthood. But maybe Mammuthus primigenius had a much shorter growth period.

(At the moment, the sheer glory of viewing his 'creation' had eclipsed the feelings of cold here in the lab. Milton Ambrose no longer noticed that his breath was a white mist in front of his face or that the air in here felt cold in his lungs.

"Hey, Snuffy, here's your dinner," Paula said, appearing beside Dr. Ambrose with a huge wheeled tub full of food—grass, mushrooms, seaweed, and moss—which she indicated to the mammoth.

Snuffy trumpeted happily at the sight of his food

Milton Ambrose helped Paula open up the animal's cage and they both walked inside to feed it, with Paula wheeling the tub in front of her.

There was no danger. The reason Snuffy was inside a cage at all was because the anterior part of the chamber contained scientific equipment that the mammoth could easily damage if permitted to walk around unrestrained.

Snuffy followed them obediently over to where Paula parked his tub of compounded feed. Then he waited patiently until both the doctor and his assistant had stepped back before lumbering forward and dipping his trunk into the trough.

Paula had mixed in the orange food supplements with the rest of the food. After she and the doctor watched the mammoth lift several mouthfuls of food up to his mouth with his trunk, they both retreated out of the cage, with Paula pulling the now-empty tub that she'd fed it from last time after her.

Dr. Ambrose locked the cage after them.

"There's something that's been bothering me," Paula said as they both walked past the machines in the anterior part of the enclosure. "Something that doesn't exactly make sense."

"What's that?" Milton Ambrose asked. "So long as it doesn't involve that crazy bitch Ray Linn, I don't mind listening."

Paula laughed at the mention of Ray Linn's name. "Sir, you really hate Ray, don't you?"

He scowled back at her. "Doesn't everyone hate that insufferable woman?"

Paula shook her head. "Personally, I find her amusing with her endless 'Woke' rants."

Dr. Ambrose's laughter as they stepped outside was only a few degrees warmer than Snuffy's enclosure. "That's because you don't have to deal with her, Paula. Take it from me: if you had to meet with Ray Linn on a regular basis, you'd dislike her even more than I do."

Paula locked the door to Snuffy's enclosure. She and Dr. Ambrose locked up the lab and walked together towards the exit.

"I'm glad that we've so far managed to keep Snuffy a secret from Ray Linn," Dr. Ambrose told Paula as they exited the building. "Only heaven knows what PR damage she could do to us if she ever discovered we've got a 'living fossil' here on our premises."

"Yes indeed," Paula quickly agreed. "But, doctor, that wasn't what I meant was bothering me."

He paused in the corridor to hear her out. "Oh? My apologies then, Paula. It's just that each time I think of Ray Linn, my irritation boils over. So, what exactly is bothering you?"

"Well . . ." Paula's face squeezed up in a frown. ". . . I'm still unable to understand why since awakening Snuffy, we've been unable to bring any other animals back to life."

Dr. Ambrose's irritation faded as he considered the problem along with her. "I know what you mean," he said with a heavy sigh. "Aside from our success with our woolly friend, we're still only able to revive bugs—cockroaches and houseflies—and those for just five minutes or so."

Paula nodded. "My assumption was always that what worked for larger animals would work for the smaller ones too—our lab rats and mice and maybe rabbits even."

Faced with this familiar problem, Dr. Ambrose relaxed. While he and Paula Helmsworth made their way over to the front F-Bio parking lot, he explained: "Well, you need to understand that we had an immense amount of luck with reviving Snuffy. In fact, now I'm tempted to believe that our mammoth friend may not have been dead at all when we got him, but that he'd somehow been trapped in a state of suspended animation for all of those thousands of years. You know, alive, but seemingly dead for all that time."

"Suspended animation, like in sci-fi movies? But, sir, is that really possible?"

"Well, it's a good guess anyway, and it fits the facts. Of course, there may be other explanations."

CHAPTER 6

". . . And so, my dear brothers and sisters, I both implore and encourage you all to walk your Christian walk guided by our Lord Jesus's exhortation to love others as we love ourselves."

This statement concluded Rev. Luke Jones's sermon for that Sunday morning. After a brief word of prayer, Rev. Jones backed off from the podium and handed the service over to one of his deacons.

Seated beside his wife Charlotte in the First Baptist Church, Gary Bentley sang and prayed along with the rest of the congregation. The church building was about half-full this Sunday morning, which was normal.

"Nice sermon," he told Charlotte as the ushers passed the offering tray around. "Luke really hit the nail on the head with that one."

Charlotte Bentley nodded back at him. "I feel blessed today."

Gary smiled his agreement, and as the offering tray reached him and Charlotte, he reached into his pocket for his wallet.

Gary Bentley attended church occasionally. Years ago, Charlotte had forced him to come to services with her, but nowadays he came for his own reasons, which was mostly that being in church filled him with the kind of peace he never felt anywhere else.

Which is great, 'cos each morning when I wake up, the damn world seems more bent on spiraling completely out of control.

Gary looked at his watch. The time was almost 11 a.m. Today, he was working an afternoon shift.

Lots of time before then, he thought with a smile.

***

17

The church service ended and, alongside Charlotte, Gary walked up to the front of the church to say hello to the pastor. He and Luke were good friends.

"I didn't see you here last week," Luke told Gary after they'd shook hands. He was a stout man with a broad smile and a deep belly laugh.

Gary looked apologetic. "Ah, you know how it is, brother. Sometimes I gotta hold my church service in the woods with the woodland critters."

They laughed at his reference to his job.

Then the church secretary interrupted them. Gary waited while the little old lady urgently whispered something into Luke's ears.

Luke nodded to her and then turned back to Gary and Charlotte. "Folks, you'll have to excuse me." But then he seemed to remember something, because he added. "No, don't leave yet. I've a present for you, Gary."

Gary gave the preacher a confused look. "What is it?"

But Rev. Luke Jones was already hurrying off after the church secretary. "I'll meet you both outside in about ten minutes." He laughed. "What I've got for you ain't something I should hand over in God's house."

***

Outside, in the church parking lot, with autumn leaves falling around them, Gary unwrapped the suspicious-looking bundle the church pastor had handed him.

Then he gasped. "Wow, where the he—" (he stopped himself from swearing just in time) "Where'd you get this?"

Luke's present to Gary was a Weatherby Mark V hunting rifle. The 300 Magnum gleamed in the warm midday sun.

A broad smile crept over Gary's face as he studied the firearm. He'd wanted one of these for ages for his gun collection.

Rev. Luke Jones was himself a hunter, and he and Gary often went out in the woods for target practice, or to bag themselves some venison during hunting season.

Charlotte frowned and glanced around at the dispersing church conversation. The gun her husband was studiously examining made her feel self-conscious. "I see what you meant that it's something you couldn't hand over in church," she said. "Where'd you buy it, Luke? It looks old and expensive."

Luke Jones laughed. "Oh, I didn't buy it. You both know Maggie Olsen's father passed away recently. Well, the gun was his. After trying it out a couple times, she decided the caliber was far too much for her liking, and thought that a large burly guy like me would handle its recoil better."

Gary smiled. "You know I really can't picture a small woman like Sister Olsen using this to shoot anything. It'd probably dislocate her shoulder."

Luke nodded. "Yeah, she thought so too. So, she hands it to me, and then I remembered what you, Gary, said to me two months ago when we was out in the woods together, 'bout how you'd like one for your gun collection . . ."

Gary nodded as the recollection returned. "Yeah, and to possibly ward off the biggest of bears around these woods."

"Hey, don't you dare shoot any bears with that thing!" Charlotte instantly objected.

Both men burst out laughing.

"Relax, honey," Gary told her after he and the pastor had laughed for a good while. "We hardly get any bears in the campgrounds." Then he tapped the wooden stock of the Weatherby. "But still, it's good firepower to carry around. Way more accurate than a shotgun, too."

"Oh, I almost forgot," Luke Jones said. "Sister Olsen also gave me a box of cartridges for it—those heavy duty 300 Weatherby Magnums. Hold on a moment while I get them for you."

He hurried off towards the parsonage.

Gary wrapped the gun up again and smiled at Charlotte.

She frowned back at him. "I mean it, Gary. If you dare shoot any bears with that thing, don't you dare come back home."

Still smiling, Gary stashed the Weatherby in the backseat of the pickup truck and waited for Luke to return with the bullets for it.

***

Later that afternoon, as Gary cleaned the Weatherby Mark V on the tailgate of his pickup truck, his thoughts drifted to the stories he'd heard over the years. The strange noises campers reported deep in the woods, the sightings of animals larger than they should be—he always wrote them off as tall tales or misidentifications.

He ran a cloth down the barrel, inspecting the rifle's polished surface. He had a feeling, deep in his gut, that the peace of this quiet little town was about to be shattered.

As evening fell, Gary stood at the edge of his property, staring out into the shadowy tree line, his rifle resting on his shoulder. The sun sank behind the mountains, casting long, eerie shadows over the forest floor. Somewhere in those depths, something moved. He could feel it. A shift in the wind, a distant rustle of leaves, but there was something more. His instincts, honed by years of patrolling the woods, were on high alert. A creeping tension wound through his muscles as he scanned the horizon. "If something's out there," he muttered to himself, gripping the rifle tighter, "I'll be ready." But even as the words left his lips, he knew that whatever was coming, it was unlike anything he had ever faced before.

CHAPTER 7

Midmorning on Monday, Ray Linn drove her car up to the front gate of the F-Bio Facility.

She smiled when she noticed that the guard who'd left the guard post to attend to her was one she'd not encountered before.

"Good morning, sir," the young man greeted her pleasantly. "Do you have an appointment to—"

"My pronouns are 'she' and 'they,' " Ray quickly cut him off. "I'm not male, I am female."

The guard froze in surprise, the smile melting from his face as he did a double take and realized that even though Ray had decidedly masculine features, 'she' was wearing a skirt suit.

"I'm sorry, sir, but I thought—"

"How dare you misgender me again," Ray angrily corrected him. "I've just told you that my pronouns are 'she' and 'they.' I insist that you use those while either addressing or referring to me. I'm here to see Dr. Milton Ambrose. Rest assured that I'm going to have a word with him about your disrespectful behavior."

The young guard looked confused.

"Well, don't stand there looking like a turd. Are you going to let me in or not? I'm with the USDA and APHIS and I'm here to inspect your facility."

"Yes, of course, si—I mean, ma'am," the guard sputtered. "Just gimme a minute to confirm your appointment.

The perplexed young man ran off into the guard post. Ray Linn smiled coldly as she saw him conversing with a second guard.

Damn rube shitheads don't seem to understand that these are woke times, she thought. *The sooner I shut this place down, the better for the modern world.*

The second guard had meanwhile come to the window of the guard post. This was someone she'd had dealings with before.

"Oh, good morning, Ms. Linn," the man said with a nervous smile.

"Well, are you going to let me in or not?" Ray asked without acknowledging his greeting. "Or do I go back to headquarters and report that I was both insulted by the staff and refused access to check on your Weapons of Mass Animal Destruction?"

The guard controlled his anger. "Of course, ma'am. I'm assuming you have an appointment to see Dr. Ambrose."

Ray Linn shook her head. "No, this is a surprise visit, so you won't have time to hide anything. Now, please let me in."

The guard sighed, but managed not to roll his eyes at her. Then he turned to the new guard. "Raise the bar, Tom."

He turned back to Ray Linn. "You need to forgive the kid. He's new here. Doesn't know who you are."

"If he ever misgenders me again, I'll report him for sexual harassment," Ray Linn told the man, as the bar lifted.

Without waiting, for a reply, she drove into the premises.

Ray Linn smiled to herself. She'd won her first woke victory of the day.

***

Although Ray Linn (born Raymond Leonard) looked like a man, 'she' 'identified' as a woman.

However, unlike most transgender and transvestite individuals who at least made an effort to physically conform to the gender they identified with, Ray had so far done no such thing.

To everyone except herself, she looked like a man wearing women's clothing. She kept her face shaved and got her hair styled, but that was as far as she went toward conforming to accepted feminine appearance.

As a result, she got misgendered on a regular basis, which was the whole intent of keeping her appearance like it was.

Ray Linn liked being misgendered. It enabled her to impose her view of the world on people.

***

Just like Ray Linn had informed the new guard at the F-Bio gate, she worked for the United States Department of Agriculture (USDA) Animal and Plant Health Inspection Service (APHIS).

Her job was to inspect research facilities in out-of-the-way places to ensure they conformed to the laid down federal standards for the treatment of animals.

Originally stationed in Washington D.C., for the past four months Ms. Linn had been in West Virginia, where her spies had assured her that at several obscure research facilities, the US Government was conducting cruel clandestine experiments on animals.

One of the research facilities fingered by Ray's spies was F-Bio.

***

Ray parked and entered the smaller of the two F-Bio buildings.

Those F-Bio staff members that she encountered on her way to Dr. Ambrose's laboratory, either avoided locking eyes with her or mumbled indistinct greetings and then hurried away from her.

No one here liked Ray. Awash in a sea of entitlement, she generally treated people like they were animals, and treated animals like they were stepping stones.

Stepping stones to her personal advancement, that is.

Her animal inspections were fair enough. She never gave a bad report if there was no cause for one, and yet her primary reason for doing her job so well was to make a name for herself.

So far, Ray had shut down three research institutes which hadn't adhered to the federal guidelines for the treatment of animals 'participating in research.'

But none of those companies had been as big as F-Bio.

Ray realized that if she could shut down F-Bio, her reputation in Washington political circles would be set in stone.

And this was the reason why, despite all evidence to the contrary, she continued to badger F-Bio.

I'm certain there's something illegal going on in this place, and I'm going to find out what it is, she told herself regularly.

Yes, Ray Linn was desperate to shut down the Futures Bioresearch facility.

And to that end, she'd placed a spy here at F-Bio, with instructions to keep watch on things and let her know immediately if anything suspicious happened.

She looked forward to the day when she'd have the termination of F-Bio on her work résumé.

CHAPTER 8

That same Monday morning, forest ranger Gary Bentley was making his rounds of the Sleepaway Campground.

Today, Gary felt that the falling leaves made a nice kaleidoscope of color. The sun was bright, the sky was blue. All in all, it was a nice morning; one in which trouble seemed far away.

The partial denuding of the trees also meant better visibility into the forest while he made his rounds. In this autumn season, Gary often didn't need to patrol both sides of the river. From either side, he could see clean through to the other, so long as there were no tree trunks in the way, that is.

Gary was walking east along the main trail to the campground parking lot when, all of a sudden, he heard loud rock music coming from the direction of the river.

Looking over there, he made out a large group of about twenty or so people standing near the river.

Their presence at the campground surprised him.

What the hell's going on over there? This is Monday. Most folks do their camping on the weekends. He winced at the loudness of the music. *And, haven't those lot ever heard of noise pollution? They're almost as bad as regular litterers.*

Gary picked up the pace and turned off the park into the trees.

In a short while he was close enough to the gathering to see men working movie cameras. There was also a wooden soundstage on which a band were playing.

Oh, looks like they're making a music video!

By now a few of the gathered people had noticed Gary. However, the attention of most of the crowd of twenty or so onlookers was riveted on the performers.

The band was all dressed in black leather, and their female lead singer and backup vocalist both had red stars painted around their left eyes.

After exchanging nods with those people who'd noticed him, Gary joined the group and watched the band mime the song, while a short and animated man gave them silent instructions.

Up this close to the huge speakers, the music was phenomenally loud. Gary felt like he was being kicked in the chest by the kick drum, and the guitars seemed to live somewhere inside his head, while the bass made him feel like he had the runs.

The lead singer sang:

"Meet me in the woods, honey,

And I'll show you what sort of animal I am.

After tonight you'll know the real meaning of 'wildlife.'

The real meaning of wildlife!"

The female lead singer had a great voice. Her voice sounded familiar to Gary, and she looked familiar also. Gary, who didn't know many modern pop or rock bands (his musical tastes were rooted firmly in 80s 'hair band' stadium rock), wondered how this band sounded so familiar to him.

It's like I know them somehow, but how?

The song wound down to a fade out.

"Okay, that was great, guys," the director told the band. Then he noticed Gary, and added: "Hey, take five, everyone. We've got official company."

Gary now felt everyone's eyes on him.

"Morning, guys," he said, "I'm forest ranger Gary Bentley. Damn, this music sure is loud. Great song, but if you keep playing it at that volume, you're gonna scare all the bears out of West Virginia."

Everyone laughed and the band walked over to meet him.

"The music has to be loud enough so we can feel it," one of the guitarists explained."

The lead singer nodded. "Yes, since we're miming the song, we ain't getting the real live vibe, so it helps, if you get my meaning."

Gary nodded too. Everyone here was in their early to mid-twenties. He was aware that to all of these young people he must look like their dad.

They're all about my son Matt's age. Oh, that's it, that's how I know them all.

"Sir, my name's Gideon Thorne," the director introduced himself. "I'm directing a music video—"

Gary nodded. "And the band is called Cherry Soufflé. That's right, ain't it?"

All of the young people stared at him in surprise.

"You've heard of us?" the lead singer asked in astonishment. "You're a fan of our music?"

Gary laughed. "My son Mike is. He's got posters of you guys on his bedroom wall. Before he thankfully went off to Penn State, he'd almost blast his mom and me out of the house playing your tunes. I don't think I ever heard him play this one though."

"This song is new," the lead singer said with a smile. "And since it's called 'Meet Me in the Woods, Honey,' Gideon had the bright idea of making the video in the real-world woods."

Gary looked at the director, who nodded and gesticulated. "Yes, yes, yes. I want true art. I need that realistic vibe, not green-screening it like everyone and their grandmother does nowadays."

Gary nodded. "Well, best of luck to you all, but I hope you do have the proper permits to film here, or else I'm gonna have to run you off the property."

There followed a brief pause while the director called out: "Hey, Stash, you did apply for permission to film out here, didn't you?"

Stash was a tall and bony young man. Seeing him instantly made Gary think of drugs; like this young guy was dealing pot or something else.

Well, they're a rock band, he reasoned. *Smoking a little weed or doing a few lines of coke seem to be part of the requirements to be in their profession.*

Stash walked over. He seemed rather apprehensive to be near Gary; like the forest ranger represented the law and he was certain to be found guilty of something or other once a close investigation of his person was made.

Remembering all of the trouble drug dealers had caused him in these same woods, Gary checked Stash's eyes for traces of any orange coloring. There were none, so he relaxed.

At least he ain't dealin' Agent Orange. Gary quickly looked around the assembled youths. Though several of them looked more than a little stoned, none of them had orange-tinted eyes, so he relaxed.

There's no trouble here.

"What's that you were asking 'bout?" Stash asked them all.

"The ranger wants to know if we got permits to use this place," the lead singer told him.

Stash scratched his head. "Well . . . yeah I know I applied for permission." He seemed to rack his memory, then he nodded. "Yeah, yeah, we're cool being here. What happened was, one of the guys at City Hall called me back on the phone and told us we could go ahead and make our video here." After looking rather confused again for a further few seconds, Stash added: "He did warn us not to litter or start any forest fires though, or the rangers would kick us out. Oh, yeah, and he told us to watch out for bears."

Everyone looked at Gary, who nodded back at them.

"Well, I guess you're good then," he said with a smile. He gestured backward with his thumb, out towards the camping trails and parking lot. "I'd better continue making my inspections."

Then he froze and smiled at the band. "Hey, guys, can you film a short video with me for my son? He'll be thrilled that I got to meet you all!"

"Shouldn't be a problem," Gideon said and then looked questioningly at the band.

"Sure, why not?" someone said. "We'll give him a shout-out. What's his name again?"

"Michael Bentley."

The guitarists picked up their guitars and then the entire band clustered around Gary and posed while making devil's-hand signs.

"Hey, Mike Bentley, this is Cherry Soufflé!" the lead singer called out in a sing-song voice, while their video director filmed everything on Gary's cellphone. "Thanks for supporting our music! Rock on!"

"Thanks, guys, I really appreciate this," Gary told the band afterward. "Have a great day!"

"You too, sir!"

Gary walked off with a smile on his face. By the time he'd returned to the camping trail, the loud music had started up again.

"Yeah, those kids are gonna drive all of the darn bears out of West Virginia if they keep those sound levels up," he said aloud. "Raccoons and foxes too, from the sound of it."

CHAPTER 9

When Ray Linn arrived in his laboratory, Dr. Ambrose sighed and tried to keep a poker face. He'd not been expecting her at all, and after the security guards had alerted him to her presence on the premises, he'd had scant time to get things in order for her arrival.

Principal amongst these preparations was the activation of a switch that rotated the anterior chamber of Snuffy's enclosure. Once this rotation was accomplished, the entire wall of the lab at that point was replaced by animal cages, while the enclosure entrance now opened into a storage room with boxes and crates piled to the ceiling, which was explained to be the case all the way to the end of Snuffy's massive Quonset hut.

The switch that caused this rotation of the wall, also lowered soundproofed louvers over the windows of the Quonset hut, so even when the mammoth inside trumpeted, there was no chance of its being heard from the outside.

The final step in the concealment was for Paula and some of the staff in the adjoining laboratories to hurriedly move some of their own research animals into the cages that had just come out of the walls.

At first, these government-suggested precautions had seemed excessive to Dr. Ambrose. But since making the acquaintance of Ms. Linn, he'd come to view them as a gift from God.

Along with Paula, Dr. Ambrose quietly followed their annoying bureaucratic visitor as she walked along the row of cages, inspecting the rabbits and monkeys. He sensed her disappointment at how calm and relaxed the animals were.

He knew she was now clutching at straws to attempt to shut F-Bio down. It bothered him however, that each time Ray visited F-Bio, she spent a disproportionate amount of time in his own laboratory.

Either she suspects that we're hiding something big in that supposed 'storage space,' or she's got a thing for me.

He studied the male 'woman' by his side, this muscular trans person who looked like one of his male staff, and cringed at the thought that 'she' might be romantically interested in him. *Heaven forbid that that be the case!*

Afterward, they sat at his table.

"I really don't see why you had to come here unannounced today," Dr. Milton Ambrose told Ray without bothering to hide his anger. "You inspected us just last week. Pardon me for saying so, but these unscheduled visits of yours are disrupting our work."

"I see that you've so far not implemented my suggestion to adjust the male slash female slash transgender ratio amongst your staff," Ray replied as if she'd not heard his complaint. However, she had a smile on her face, which showed she was delighted to have something to bitch about.

"Well, that's not really my fault," he replied. "Being from Washington, you're surely aware of all the ongoing budget cuts for government-funded research. We'd hire more people if we could, but how are we going to pay them all?"

"Where there's a will, there's always a way. You'll have money to hire both cis and trans women if you fire some of your patriarchy."

Dr. Ambrose sighed and asked Paula to fetch them coffee. This looked to be a miserable morning.

***

While listening to his unwanted 'non-binary' guest rant at him, Dr. Milton Ambrose was struck with the irony of it all, that such a stupid person, a woman—

31

No, not a woman, he thought vehemently. *I'm not drinking any of that woke Kool-Aid. She's a man, 'she' has a penis and 'she' looks and talks and even WALKS like a man. Waking up one morning and deciding that you're a woman doesn't make you one!*

As it was, Dr. Ambrose knew that many of the F-Bio staff referred to Ray Lin as 'Ms. Pronouns' when she wasn't with earshot.

Dr. Ambrose was miserably struck by the terrible irony that such a stupid person as Ms. Ray Linn could be given authority over sensible and productive members of society.

"The *woman* is worse than an airhead," he'd complained over the phone to Senator Tom McHardy, one of two senators representing West Virginia in Congress. "At least airheads aren't *naturally* dangerous; yes, they stumble and fall, but do so innocently. But Ray Linn has no innocence to her antics. Tom, have you seen her TV interviews? She *actively* promotes stupid thinking. How the hell can such a *woman*—no, such a *person*—be allowed to waltz into F-Bio— knowing the sort of covert research Washington has us doing for them—and threaten to shut us down?"

Senator McHardy had laughed. "Relax, Milt. She's full of hot air. You know that. But she's Senator Leonard's kid brother—sorry, I meant to say kid *sister*—and seeing as he doesn't want her on his own staff, we had to find something else for her to do. The USDA had an opening for a mid-level manager/standards inspector and we thought it was a harmless enough position for her. We had no idea we were giving her the clearance to stick her nose into everyone's business."

Milton Ambrose had sighed. "The bitch takes herself seriously. She's just had an argument over her rights to use the women's toilets."

"Oh, leave her be," had been the senator's reply. "She doesn't have the power to shut you down. She thinks she does, but she doesn't. But you can't throw her out either; you have to tolerate her. Sooner or later Ray will tire of investigating F-Bio and take her ass off somewhere where she'll be no bother to you. But for the time being, just ensure that you keep all of your most important research well away for her. Like that revived mammoth, for instance. The president still isn't sure how we're gonna handle revealing it to the public. We don't want an idiot like Ray whistleblowing it before we're ready."

***

Knowing that F-Bio couldn't be shut down by Ray Linn was, however, little comfort when faced with the 'woman' herself.

Am I the only one who notices that this person's name 'Ray Linn' sounds just like 'railing,' as in, 'complain bitterly?' Milton Ambrose wondered.

After two more hours of her companionship, in which Ray did her best to convince him that two plus two wasn't always four, that gender identity was a state of mind and not of body, and finally, that there was nothing whatsoever wrong with genetic males who'd not yet had hormone treatment and Gender Reassignment Surgery competing in women's sports, even in the boxing and wrestling events, Ray announced that she needed to use the restroom.

Paula sighed on hearing this while Dr. Ambrose cringed.

Ray, however, had already gotten up to her feet. "I'll be right back. If I remember correctly, it's right down the corridor and to the left?"

"Paula will take you," Dr. Ambrose replied in a defeated voice.

Then, after the pair left his laboratory, he stared long and hard at the door through which they'd exited.

She's going to use the restroom merely to make a fuss. She's going to use the female restroom and not the male one, and if anyone comments, she's going to say they're misgendering her again, and then she'll complain to her superiors that we're not a woke and trans-friendly work environment. How the hell are we supposed to be trans-friendly when we don't have any transgender employees?

Fortunately, there was no ugly bathroom encounter today.

Apparently, word had spread far and wide in the facility that Ray Linn was around, and everyone was doing their best to avoid her woke presence.

CHAPTER 10

After dinner that evening, completely unaware that, block by block, a massive disaster that would involve him was once more building up, Gary Bentley told his wife Charlotte about his meeting with the rock band Cherry Soufflé.

She laughed. "You mean the ones on Mike's wall?"

He nodded. "The very same." He got out his phone and found the shout-out video the band had recorded for their son. "Here, look at this!"

Charlotte watched the video clip and then grinned. "Well, they seem like a nice lot after all. If they weren't so damn noisy tho'."

Gary said, "I suspect they only seem noisy 'cause we're getting on in years, and our ears ain't what they used to be. Lots of those concerts we attended back in the day had some really loud music happening."

"Maybe that's the case," Charlotte agreed. "I recall watching Smashing Pumpkins at Lollapalooza and thinking I'd go deaf. Hey, have you sent Mike a copy yet?"

Gary shook his head. "I haven't had the time or the network reception. You know how sketchy internet coverage is out in the woods."

Charlotte nodded. "Maybe the phone companies should look into that. But then, maybe not. Who's gonna be calling from there? The raccoons?"

Gary laughed and sent the Cherry Soufflé shout-out video to his son, who soon replied with huge emojis of surprise and a large "DAD, YOU'RE THE GREATEST!"

Gary turned to show Mike's reply to Charlotte.

Charlotte wasn't looking at him, however. She was turning up the volume on the TV.

"What's that?"

"Shush! Just watch," she replied with a finger to her lips.

Together, they watched. It was some kind of science program, with photographs of DNA strands placed opposite photos of animals. The image of a woman in a lab coat was superimposed between both sets of images.

"Current advances in science suggest that it's merely a matter of time before we can create accurate clones of long-vanished creatures," the female scientist was saying. "In this sense, we'll be able to make those animal species un-extinct again."

The onscreen image altered to show a 3-D image of a funny-looking bird, with the explaining scientist now inset to its right.

"This is the dodo," the woman explained. "That most famous of extinct animals, so much so that it's given us the expression 'As dead as the dodo.' But now, scientists are assuring us that, due to the wonders of science, dodos may soon be alive in our zoos again."

She nodded, and the image beside her changed to show a 3-D representation of a woolly mammoth, set against the icy backdrop of the arctic tundra.

"A second candidate for reversed extinction, or de-extinction, is the woolly mammoth. Whereas the Dodo only went into oblivion merely five hundred years ago, the wooly mammoth hasn't been around for four millennia. Imagine what a thrill it will be for them to once more walk the face of our planet.

The screen image shifted to show an animal like a mountain lion, but subtly different, with stripes on its back.

"The Tasmanian tiger is the third most popular suggested species that modern researchers have an interest in reviving. Also recently extinct, this species . . ."

As the woman continued speaking, Gary turned to Charlotte, who turned the TV volume down so she could pay attention to him instead.

Gesturing sideways at the TV, Gary said, "This is always how trouble starts when egghead nerds start playing God. First thing we saw was a dodo, which is harmless enough and might even give chickens a run for their money in the food stakes. Next we saw the mammoth, which looks cute and cuddly like that thing on Sesame Street. Mr. Snuffle—something or other."

"I think it was Mr. Snuggleoctopus," Charlotte said with a loud giggle while snuggling up close to him. "Something like that anyway."

"Yeah," Gary agreed, relaxing as her soft body pressed against his. "Anyway, that one also looks cute and harmless enough. But, Charlotte, honey, look at this damn tiger thing. Just looking at that animal, you know it's gonna make trouble for everyone the moment it comes out of whatever mechanical womb the scientists incubate it in."

Charlotte laughed and punched his arm. "Honey, you're so funny. The tigers don't look that frightening to me. They seem less dangerous than the mammoths."

Gary shook his head at her. "Uh-uh. The very word 'tiger' symbolizes danger. Mammoths are nothing but hairy elephants—they're herbivores. Tigers, on the other hand, are carnivores—they eat meat and are thus more likely to attack and kill people."

Charlotte thought about that for a long moment. "Well, anyway," she said afterward, "neither species can stand up to modern weapons, so humans have little to be afraid of from them. According to you, that gun Reverend Luke gave you as a gift should blow even the mammoth away." Then, she gave him an inquiring look. "Where'd you put the damn gun anyway? I haven't seen it in here anywhere."

"The Weatherby Mark V is still outside in the pickup truck," Gary grumbled. "I ain't brought it into the house yet cuz I don't want you startin' up about me killing innocent bears again."

"You can bring it in," Charlotte said. "At least, if it's here inside the house, you can't be killing any harmless animals in the woods with it."

Gary Bentley winced, then forced a smile. "Let the Weatherby sleep outside tonight, honey. I'll bring it in the house tomorrow."

Still unaware of the trouble brewing, Gary resumed watching TV, and finally he and Charlotte went up to bed.

CHAPTER 11

At about a quarter to midnight, Paula Helmsworth pulled up at the F-Bio front gates in her Toyota sedan.

Paula was well-known to the guards, so they saw nothing strange about her being here at so late an hour after Dr. Milton Ambrose and most of the other staff had gone home.

After explaining to them that she'd absentmindedly forgotten to feed several precious lab animals, the guards raised the security bar to let Paula into the premises.

Although the front parking lot was vacant at this hour, Paula drove around the building to the rear parking lot.

She'd told the security guards the truth about her reasons for returning to the facility this late at night.

Yes, she had neglected to feed Snuffy before leaving work. But she'd done so intentionally, so that she'd have valid cause to return here now.

In the rear parking lot, Paula parked her old sedan close to Lab 7 and the long domelike enclosure that housed Snuffy the woolly mammoth.

Maybe I shouldn't be doing this, she thought. *But I guess it's too late now to change my mind.*

Sighing deeply, Paula activated the lever that opened the trunk of her car. After ensuring that there was no around watching her, she got out and hurried around to the trunk.

"Okay, you can get out now," she told Ray Linn.

Ray Linn pushed the trunk of the car fully open and climbed out.

"You're an absolute crap driver, honey," Ray told Paula when she was properly on her feet again. "Riding in the back here, I thought my brains would be knocked out of my head by such a bumpy ride."

"I got you here, didn't I?" Paula spat back angrily. "You should be grateful to me for helping you."

Ray smirked. Tonight, she was dressed all in black. It seemed to Paula like she'd watched 'Mission: Impossible' before selecting her clothes.

"You're helping me spy on your friends because I'm paying you lots of money to do so," Ray told Paula. "Don't pretend that you like me any more than they do."

"You're a bitch."

"And you're betraying your friends for cash, honey. That makes us the same nasty kind of woman."

Paula winced angrily on hearing the totally male Ray refer to 'herself' as a 'woman.' But she didn't reply.

Ray Linn was telling the truth. For the past few months, Ray had been paying Paula Helmsworth a thousand dollars a month to keep an eye on her colleagues and her bosses.

Paula liked making the extra income, and besides, Ray had promised Paula that after she shut down F-Bio, she'd hire Paula as her personal assistant, which meant they'd travel the country together, shutting offending institutions down.

Paula liked working here at F-Bio, but with Ray's persistent negativity and scheming against it, she'd begun considering her current place of employment a sinking ship.

And so, while Paula hoped that Ray wouldn't succeed in shutting down F-Bio, she nonetheless thought it wise to remain on Ray's good side.

That's if she has one, Paula thought grimly. Then she gestured over to Ray. "Wait over there by the Quonset. I'll open up one of the lab windows and let you in."

CHAPTER 12

"I'll be both delighted and promoted once this place is out of business," Ray Lin told Paula once the latter had let her into Lab 7.

She felt a tingling of delight at being here. This was how things were meant to be done. Paula had promised to show her something incredible tonight, and yet hadn't said exactly what it was, just that there was a huge animal here in the lab that was in need of saving.

Now that they were inside the laboratory, however, Paula seemed to be having a change of heart. She seemed nervous in the extreme, so much so that she was lighting up a joint to calm herself.

"So, honey, where is this endangered species of yours?" Ray asked in a saccharine voice. "Is it upstairs?"

Paula laughed and puffed marijuana smoke right in Ray's face. "No, it's a lot closer to us than you can possibly imagine. Look around you. Don't you notice anything different about this lab tonight?"

Ray looked around her. She wondered what Paula was getting at.

This building looks exactly the same as it did when I was here this morning No, it's different in some way.

It took a long while before Ray worked out the difference. She agreed that she wasn't the smartest woman around. But brains never really mattered anyway. The endless male acquisition of trophy wives proved as much.

No, what really matters in life is getting results. And getting 'results' results from taking action.

Ray was a man/woman of action.

"I see nothing different, Paula," she informed Paula angrily. "Stop messing with me."

"Use your eyes, man," Paula replied.

Ray's eyes instantly narrowed. "How dare you call me a 'man.' I'm not a man. My pronouns are—"

"Yeah, yeah, I know, man. But just look around and work out what's not the same anymore in here. And don't give me any bitchy looks. I'm not gonna help you any."

Now that the marijuana was at work in her body, Paula clearly wasn't overly bothered by Ray's caustic attitude. "You're supposed to be so good at sniffing oddities out," she added. "So, Sherlock, what's different about this room now?"

"Just tell me."

Paula shook her head and blew out more smoke. "No, figure it out for yourself."

Ray considered taking the joint away from Paula, and then knocking some sense into the girl. Though she identified as a woman, she didn't mind the strength advantage her male genes gave her, particularly when it came down to bitch-slapping sense into a cis-woman.

But just before Ray Linn might have gotten violent with Paula, she understood what Paula was getting at.

"That wall over there," she said with a tremor in her voice. "It looks different now. Where the fuck did that door come from? What happened to the cages and the animals that were there this morning?"

"Bingo, you win the grand prize!" Paula said. "Fake wall, like a magic trick. What I want you to see is behind that door over there. Hey, man, hold on," she added as Ray set off for the door in question.

"Yes," Ray asked impatiently. "And for heaven's sake—will you stop calling me 'Man!' "

"Sure thing, man," Paula replied with an amused laugh. "What I wanna tell you is, before you open that door over there, you need to put on one of those thermal jumpsuits hanging by the door."

"What the hell for?" Ray demanded of her stoned companion, greatly angered by her misgendered pronouns.

"Man, either suit up, or else freeze your ass off in there," Paula replied with blithe unconcern about how angry Ray was. "Go, go, go! I need to get some stuff out of this safe over here and then I'll join you in there."

"This had better not be a trick," Ray said as she began suiting up.

Paula burst out laughing. "Oh, it ain't no trick. Your life is unlikely to remain the same once you've met Snuffy."

Ray wanted to ask her some more questions, but then she realized she was simply wasting time.

The silly girl keeps repeating that what she brought me here to see is right behind this door here. Better I finish suiting up and then investigate it instead of wasting time with stoned ass!

So, Ray quickly dressed up and then opened the beckoning door and stepped inside.

And once Ray Linn reached the animal cage and saw what was in there, time seemed to stand still for her. As her breath misted before her face, she felt like she'd traveled back a million years in time.

"Oh, my dear God!" she exclaimed loudly once her awe on seeing the humongous woolly mammoth had subsided a little. "I'm gonna be famous worldwide once I expose this conspiracy!"

She got out her cellphone from her purse and began making a video of the woolly mammoth.

CHAPTER 13

Outside in the laboratory, Paula heard Ray's loud exclamation clearly

The knowledge of what she'd done made Paula feel quite bad. The joint she was smoking was, however, effectively countering her bad emotions and helping her feel mellow about the current situation.

Prior to today, Paula had not told Ray Linn anything about Snuffy because she liked the woolly mammoth a lot, and didn't want to expose it to the kind of media hassles that were certain to result from its being revealed to the public.

Snuffy is such a calm quiet beast and doesn't deserve to be manipulated by a bitch like Ray. But Ray keeps on hassling me for information and keeps telling me that she'll stop paying me if I don't feed her something good soon. Sorry, Snuffy, I didn't mean to turn on you like this.

She lit a fresh joint and turned her attention to the safe.

By now, Paula was so high that it took her ages to tap in the correct combination to open the safe up.

By the time she'd finally made her fingers do what she wanted them to, and the safe swung open, she was even more stoned than before. Now she felt like she needed to sit down and wait for her mind to clear up a bit before she got out Snuffy's food supplements.

So, she sat down and smoked weed a little longer and wound up even more stoned.

It wasn't until she became aware of Ray shaking her, that she got up again.

"Just look at you. You should be ashamed of yourself," Ray said.

"Yeah, man, I'm so ashamed that I know you," Paula said with sincere conviction. "You're such a mean person."

Then she got to her feet and walked past Ray to the safe again.

And it was now that Paula Helmsworth completely screwed up. In her mind 'up' and 'down' had become more-or-less the same thing. High on pot like she was, instead of taking the woolly mammoth's food supplements out of the safe, she instead took out two large packs of Agent Orange.

"Hey, help me get out another two," she told Ray. "The poor animal deserves a special treat tonight since I've betrayed him like this."

She watched to ensure that Ray also picked up two wrong packages and then staggered over to the enclosure entrance.

"Hey, Snuffy baby," Paula called as she walked inside. "Aunty Paula's got a surprise for you tonight."

CHAPTER 14

Ray Linn continued filming. This mammoth video was certain to go viral in minutes; in one hour, she'd be famous.

It's literally gonna be a mammoth achievement! Ha-ha-ha!

At first, Ray was impressed by how Paula didn't seem affected by the arctic climate in the enclosure. But then she smirked and thought instead: *It has to be because she's stoned. The silly girl could freeze to death in here and not notice it.*

"What the hell is this orange stuff?" Ray asked Paula as she watched her mix the orange contents of the four packages into a large wheeled tub of animal feed.

"Vitamins and . . . and antibiotics," Paula replied. "Doc doesn't want Snuffy dying on us 'cos he's not used to our modern diseases."

"Oh, okay. But aren't you using a bit too much of it?"

Paula giggled. "Use your eyes, man. Snuffy's a big boy. He can take it."

If this dumb woman calls me 'Man' one more time, I will fucking END her," Ray thought angrily. *I'll beat her to death in here, and damn the consequences!*

But she managed to calm herself again and, not desiring to be further angered by Paula's disrespect of her pronouns, left her side and walked over to stare at the caged mammoth again.

The animal was up on his feet now and was standing by the steel bars of the cage, with its huge tusks poking through the grill.

The woolly mammoth towered over Ray, but his eyes were calm and gentle. She got no impressions of this being a violent creature. She thought that he smelt like a bear.

Ray didn't know what sort of steel the cage was made of. But she doubted that it would withstand the impact if the mammoth was determined to break out of here.

She took a few more photographs with her cellphone.

Ray had all sorts of questions to ask Paula, but Paula was hardly in any state to give any really coherent answers. So, Ray Linn contented herself with plotting how she intended to use this animal's unexpected presence in here to advance herself and bring down F-Bio.

The main thing I need to do is emphasize the fact that this creature—the only one of its kind in the world—has been kept secret from everyone. The public has a right to know, don't they? Simply make this animal's presence public—

She heard Paula behind her and got out of the woman's way. She watched Paula open up the cage and wheel the tub of feed inside.

"Hey, Snuffy, sorry I'm late with your food," Paula giggled. Then she jerked a hand at the giant pachyderm, whereupon the mammoth turned around and obediently followed after her, stepping behind Paula with one enormous tusk on either side of her body.

"Hey, isn't it dangerous to be in there alone with it?" Ray asked as Paula filled the animal's feeding trough with food.

"Nah, Snuffy's as gentle as a lamb." Paula gestured to Ray. "Come on inside. You can pat him if you like."

After considering the danger of entering the cage for a while and finally deciding there was none, Ray Linn entered the mammoth's cage also.

She wanted to film some close-range video of the animal. That way, even if the US Government decided to squash her expose, the internet cryptid cults couldn't debunk the facts.

While 'Snuffy' ate his dinner and Paula lit a fresh joint, Ray recorded lots more video and continued to think on how she would use the mammoth's existence to her advantage and career advancement:

Well, first of all, this mammoth is clearly being mistreated by being kept in such constrained quarters. A beast of this size needs space in which to roam.

Additionally, there's the question of its personal hygiene. How are its toilet facilities managed?

As Ray continued filming, her excitement grew. The video would be her key to fame, her revenge against the government, and the triumph of her ideals. But as she moved closer to the massive creature, something felt wrong. Snuffy, who had initially seemed docile, let out a deep, guttural sound, low and foreboding. His enormous frame shifted uneasily, his breathing growing labored.

Ray took a cautious step back, her phone still recording, though her hands had begun to tremble. "What's wrong with it?" she whispered, turning toward Paula, who had just finished dumping the last of the orange cubes into Snuffy's feeding trough.

"Dunno." Paula's eyes were wide, but her judgment was clouded by the haze of drugs, oblivious to the fatal mistake they had just made.

CHAPTER 15

Tonight's dinner tasted funny to Snuffy. The huge animal scooped up his meal—a mixture of grasses, sedges, and edible herbs—in his trunk and transferred them into his mouth, but each chew and swallow filled it with an unusual sensation.

Snuffy the woolly mammoth was fast becoming agitated. His muscles tensed up and strange thoughts, crazy and unfamiliar imagery, filled his brain.

Snuffy wasn't any smarter than regular elephants, and, as such, had no way of knowing that the orange nuggets that he'd come to enjoy as a regular part of his meals were the cause of the problem.

All Snuffy knew was that the two humans standing next to him were irritating him.

After having been in captivity for so long, he was well acclimatized to human presence and found human company comforting, a sort of replacement for his missing herd.

But tonight, Paula and Ray's presence and voices gave Snuffy no comfort whatsoever. Their voices rang in his brain like the thunder of a storm on the prehistoric steppe-tundra.

A mammoth is a humongous creature and as such, a small amount of the crack variant called Agent Orange would hardly have made any real changes to Snuffy's metabolism.

But in her stoned state, Paula had fed the woolly mammoth about a hundred times the dose a human being would use.

And that hundredfold amount of Agent Orange was much, much more than even a mammoth could cope with. And Snuffy soon realized that he liked the taste of this new addition to his diet. Agent Orange wasn't sweet, but it had character.

The problem was that Agent Orange's 'bad character' very soon began to alter Snuffy's own gentle character in the craziest and most dangerous of ways.

As Snuffy continued feeding, his irritation with the two humans beside him grew and grew. Soon, he began considering eliminating them.

Such a murderous impulse was completely alien to the mammoth's gentle nature, but the more Agent Orange he consumed, the more he came to like the idea.

CHAPTER 16

Several kilometers away from the Futures Bioresearch buildings, the rock band Cherry Soufflé was partying it up amidst the partially autumn-colored trees of the Sleepaway Campground.

Video director Gideon Thorne had wanted some night shots of the band running through the woods in the video, and now that those were in the can, everyone had decided to spend the night camping in the woods and return to town in the morning.

'Meet Me in the Woods, Honey' was a guaranteed smash hit. No doubt about it.

The band was camped close to the river. They had several tents positioned around a large campfire. There was lots of wine and beer, and lots of food also. There were also lots of party drugs in evidence—weed and speed and coke. Just about everyone present was in a good mood and already partly stoned.

The band and their girlfriends and boyfriends were all laughing and drinking, and the hangers-on and roadies and groupies were having fun too.

About the only person not partying it up while the moon shone brightly down on their gathering, was Stash Harris, the young man whom ranger Gary Bentley had thought looked like a criminal.

***

Gary's suspicions had been spot on.

Though officially part of the Cherry Soufflé road crew, Stash Harris was also the band's drug connection. Stash was the one responsible for purchasing all of the narcotics required to keep a rock band 'rocking down the highway.'

You name it, Stash either had it, or could get it for you in a very short time.

In that sense, Stash Harris was possibly the most indispensable member of Cherry Soufflé's entourage.

***

"Here you go, bro!"

At the entrance to his tent, Stash handed a bag of rolled up marijuana joints to lead guitarist Damien Blackwood. Damien, who was already quite stoned, raised the bag up and peered myopically at it, and then asked, "Some good shit, man?"

Stash laughed. "Only the best for you, amigo."

"Yeah, yeah, dude, thanks!"

Damien high-fived Stash and then shambled back over to the campfire to sit beside his girlfriend, lead vocalist Cherry Angel, who was as stoned as he was. The pair kissed and then Damien opened up the bag of weed and began handing out joints to everyone.

Video director Gideon tried to light his joint in the campfire and almost set himself on fire, to everyone's amusement.

"We're lucky that old ranger dude can't see us now," someone said to much accompanying laughter.

"He'd accuse us of trying to poison the bears!" a woman replied, increasing the laughter around the campfire.

Stash laughed also, and took a pull from his can of beer. Stash was intentionally seated away from the others on a foldable chair by the entrance of his tent. That way, anyone who wanted some stuff could easily reach him.

His arrangement with the band was a simple one: every month or so, their manager handed Stash a twenty or thirty grand 'fun fund,' in cash, and Stash made the necessary purchases.

Stash was honest enough with the money he was given, and only took the normal dealer's cut off the top. He'd figured out he had a sweet gig here; he was making easy money, no reason to shoot himself in the pinkie toes.

Stash Harris hardly ever got high himself. He was around too many drugs and drug addicts all of the time, and was extremely wary of becoming an addict himself.

Stash almost religiously followed the maxim that dealers shouldn't get high on their own supply. To his mind, drugs were a great source of income, but not great recreation. He'd seen too many lives wasted because someone couldn't stop snorting or shooting up.

He snapped out of his reflections as a gangly rocker and a small woman walked up to him.

"I need some rocket fuel, bro," said bass player Alistair Collensworth.

"Yeah, gotta powder our noses some more," his girlfriend, backing vocalist Elara Nightshade, added.

"Coming right up," Stash told them both and ducked into his tent. The other two waited outside. It was accepted band etiquette that no one, utterly no one, ever entered Stash's quarters except if he asked them to.

From force of habit, Stash looked around to check that nothing inside his tent had been disturbed while he was outside of it. Though unlikely to happen, it wasn't unheard of for addicts to try to infiltrate his tent through the back, while he was dealing out front.

But everything was exactly how he'd left it. His tote bag full of drugs was undisturbed.

More importantly, the second package, the large bundle of Agent Orange he was scheduled to deliver to Henny and Roy Cullens, was still undisturbed too.

That was almost a hundred grand's worth of 'orange.'

Stash shivered as he stared at the innocuous-looking bundle of Agent Orange. He'd seen what the drug had done to people—he'd been present when one girl's head had literally split open and her brains—bright orange in color from being pickled by the demonic narcotic—had exploded out of her skull.

Stash had witnessed another Agent Orange addict stab his own kid in the face with a pencil simply because the boy had asked for help with his homework at the wrong time.

Hell no, Stash thought with a deeply ingrained feeling of dread. *I don't want anything more to do with that Agent Orange shit than I have to.*

Tearing his gaze away from the offensive drug package, he crawled over to his tote bag, and unzipped it. After dismissively shoving aside his black Glock 17 automatic, he found a medium-sized bag of cocaine and put it in his pocket. After a little reflection, he put two more bags of coke into his pocket also, along with two baggies of crack for drummer Silas Drayton. Finally, he got out another bag of pre-rolled ready-to-smoke joints.

"Hey, Stash, what's keepin' ya in there?" Elara called out. "You having a baby in there?"

"Maybe he's taking a shit!" her boyfriend laughed.

"I'm coming, I'm coming!" Stash called back to them, which proved to be the wrong reply to make, as a few moments later, he heard Elara remark seriously to Alistair: "Wow, he's actually jerking off in there!"

"Can't blame the dude if he is—you know his chick ain't here tonight," was Alistair's droll reply.

Stash scowled and crawled out of the tent before the pair summoned others over with their laughter.

"Here you go," he told Alistair and Elara, handing them their bag of cocaine. "Have a nice flight." As an afterthought, he handed the drummer's baggies of crack cocaine to Alistair. "Hey, pass these on to Silas for me."

"Cool, dude!" After slapping palms with Stash, the bass player and his girlfriend walked away.

Stash settled down in his chair again and resumed drinking his beer. Across from him, someone put on some music—not the band's tunes, of course, but some poppy dance music by Bad Bunny.

Once the music began, the girls all shrieked and started pulling their boyfriends away to dance or fuck in the woods.

Stash laughed as he watched the couples start splitting off.

After a few seconds reflection, he decided it would be okay to smoke a joint himself.

It's cool. I'm not due to supply Henny and Roy with their Agent Orange till the crack of dawn. My head will've cleared up by then.

Stash Harris got out a stick of marijuana and walked over to the campfire to ask someone to light him up.

The party continued long and loudly on through the night.

CHAPTER 17

Over at F-Bio, Ray Linn had finally decided she'd recorded enough video of Snuffy, and put her cell phone back into her purse.

Ray had just gotten through pumping Paula Helmsworth for information about Snuffy.

She was impressed to learn that the mammoth had been carried in here stone cold dead and frozen in amber, and that the institute's scientists had then brought the animal back to life.

For a moment, Ray's ambitious heart softened as she considered the genius of these men:

Maybe I shouldn't shut them down after all. There's so much good they can do with this revival technology.

But then, her normal way of reasoning reasserted itself:

No, no, no, I mustn't be soft here. We can't have crackpots like this playing God. What will they think to revive next? Dinosaurs, I'm sure. And then, because they've not been properly regulated by me, we'll all wind up living in a Jurassic World nightmare. And next they're certain to attempt to genetically conform the sexes into fixed binary modes. Scientists like these assholes are the exact same ones who keep telling me I'm a man because my genes are male, and that my sexual identity has nothing to do with my feelings and beliefs.

Both women were still inside of the wooly mammoth's cage. The beast itself was now fast asleep. After eating his dinner, Snuffy had walked off to the massive rock formation in the middle of the room and lay down there and shut his eyes.

The cold in the enclosure was now clearly getting to Paula, who was visibly shivering in her thin clothing but who, because of how much pot she'd smoked, seemed unaware of how cold she was.

Ray considered taking Paula outside the laboratory to continue discussing the mammoth.

Then she decided that letting Paula freeze, with the bonus possibility of her catching pneumonia, would be nice payback for the woman's insulting attitude.

A short stay in intensive care will teach her some manners.

Ray glanced over at Snuffy, who seemed to be waking up now. She was still in awe of the mammoth.

I've been near elephants before. I even rode on one when I was a little boy—no I mean little GIRL—dammit, this stoned bitch has infected me with her stupidity, she's making me misgender myself! But this thing is fucking massive. It almost looks like someone draped an endless rug over a truck!

"Listen to me," Ray told Paula. "We need to think this through. You mustn't screw this up for me . . . I mean, for us both. Do you understand?"

"Yeah, whatever you say, man."

Ray now felt too elated to care about being misgendered. But she knew Paula didn't get the full implications of anything.

As Paula got out another joint from her pocket and patted herself down for her lighter, Ray did her best to explain her plan of action to her:

"Now listen, the first thing we have to do is ensure that no one suspects that *I* know anything about this creature being here."

Paula nodded. She'd found her lighter and was about lighting up, but Ray snatched the marijuana cigarette from her fingers and threw it somewhere out of sight.

Oops, I think it landed on the mammoth. Thank God, she hadn't lit it up yet, or the beast would go up in flames and I'd never forgive myself if that happened.

Paula was glaring at her, in a stoner's passive sort of rage. "What the hell did you do that for, man?" she grumbled, while clutching at her sides and shivering badly.

"You need to both sober up and pay close fucking attention to what I'm saying," Ray said testily. "I'm explaining how we're going to handle my big reveal about your hairy friend over there."

She jerked a thumb over at Snuffy. She noticed that the mammoth was back up on his feet again, and was looking in their direction. He seemed quite tense; Ray had the clear impression of Snuffy's muscles being bunched up tightly under their covering of skin and fur.

Snuffy's eyes looked strange now. They had an orange tint to them that Ray hadn't noticed earlier.

That weird coloration must be the result all of those damn vitamins and food supplements and antibiotics that they feed the poor thing. Who the hell knows what these animals used to eat back in the day? I'm certain these crackpot scientists are poisoning the poor creature.

The mammoth's tense posture worried Ray. Paula, however, had her back to Snuffy and so couldn't see what Ray could.

The animal seems to be mulling something over, Ray thought. *That look in its eyes. If it was human, I'd say it was quite angry; enraged even. But angry about what? So far as I can see, aside from the crazy meds they're feeding it, it's got a cushy life here.*

"It's too fucking cold in here!" Paula moaned. "I can't think straight."

"Oh, alright," Ray agreed, a little upset that Paula wouldn't be catching pneumonia tonight. "Let's go out into the lab and I'll find you some coffee to drink."

"Yeah, sure, I've some more joints in my bag—"

Ray was already turning towards the cage exit. But then, out of the corner of her eye, she caught sight of a blur of motion.

She turned back to stare into the depths of the cage, saw that the mammoth was charging right at them, and attempted to flee.

However, Ray couldn't move fast enough. The mammoth came on impossibly fast, like a sports car accelerating from 0 to 60 mph in a matter of seconds. As it neared the two women, the beast seemed to grow and grow in size until its bulk filled up all of the space they could have possibly escaped to.

"Hey, don't look so worried, man," Paula was telling Ray. "I'm not gonna screw up or—"

Paula never saw what hit her, she never even suspected the danger until she died from it.

Ray very clearly saw the mammoth's immense left tusk emerge like a spear from between Paula's breasts. Paula's mouth gaped open in shock and pain.

And then the charging creature hit Ray Linn too and her world faded completely to black.

CHAPTER 18

"Oh shit!" a male voice exclaimed. "What the hell happened in here?"

"Something . . . something killed Paula!"

Then there was the sound of retching.

The voices reached Ray Lin in a far-far-off and comfortable place, where it seemed like she could sleep forever if she wanted too. Then another the first voice spoke again.

"Dude, Paula ain't the only one in here. Who's that lying over there?"

Ray had been about to open her eyes, but after that question was asked, she kept them tightly shut.

She heard the brisk step of approaching feet and relaxed her body to give the impression that she was still unconscious.

She was lying on her side, and soon felt hands roll her body over.

"You're not gonna believe this," the unknown man beside her told his equally unseen companion. "It's that bureaucrat asshole from USDA—the one that's trying to shut us down."

"Ms. Pronouns? What the hell is she doing in here? Hey, is she dead too?"

"Nah, she's still alive, but out cold."

"Shit. I wish she'd died instead of Paula."

"Me too. But you know what they say—only the good die young."

By now Ray Linn was seething with anger. *Ms. Pronouns? Is that what they call me behind my back?*

She waited until the footsteps receded several paces and then opened up her eyes a crack to survey her surroundings.

She was lying just inside of the cage door. Two security guards were bent over Paula's body, once more checking it for signs of life.

Seeing that no one was looking at her, Ray opened her eyes wider. Her body ached a lot, but a quick and quiet examination revealed she'd not broken anything.

I got lucky. The mammoth hit me and I bounced off of him and . . . Paula wasn't so lucky tho'.

Ray looked around but saw no sign of the killer mammoth.

The two security guards straightened up again. They glanced over at Ray's prone form and then looked away again.

"Okay," one of them said. "Now, we don't know what the hell they were keeping locked up in this place. But the way I figure it out, something angered it—most likely that woke creep lying cold over there abused it in some way—and then it went on a rampage and killed Paula. Then it escaped out into the woods."

"Yeah, that sums it up nicely," his companion agreed. "Those loud crashes we heard must've been when it was breaking out of here. So, what do we do?"

"This is clearly a Class-A emergency. We need to get Dr. Ambrose out here immediately. At the very least, we're gonna have to locate whatever they were housing in here. If it's killed one person it can kill more people. We don't need something deadly like that roaming the countryside."

"Okay, I'll go make the call from the guard post," his companion said. "You stay here and keep an eye on Ms. Pronouns. We need to hold her/him till the police arrive. I don't know how she broke into this place, but she might've startled Paula feeding the animal and even killed her."

"We don't know if that's what happened."

"Yeah, true. But I wouldn't put anything past that woke jerk. They might have argued about sexuality and then she snapped."

"We're wasting time here, man. Go make that phone call, and get the doctor over here."

Ray was both angry and frightened now. She'd realized that she really could be framed for murdering Paula Helmsworth.

But I didn't do anything to her! These assholes both hate me and so they're going to blame me! I need to get out of here!

She watched the man who was going to make the phone call walk away out of sight. Interestingly, he headed out of the cage through its far end. She couldn't see over there because of the rock formation in the way, but the guard's action reinforced the knowledge that Snuffy the woolly mammoth had broken out of his cage.

With her heart racing with worry, Ray watched the second guard. Convinced that she'd been knocked out cold, the man was scarcely paying any attention to her.

"Damn, it's frigging cold in here!" he muttered to himself, and walked off deeper into the cage, clearly on his way to stand by the hole the escaped animal had made, where he'd be outside in the warmer night air.

Ray didn't hesitate. Once the man was five or six yards away from her, she leapt to her feet, picked up a rock that she'd earmarked for the purpose and charged the guard.

She smacked him behind the ear with all the force of her desperation, and quite a bit of anger too.

Ms. Pronouns, huh?

The guard went down like he'd been shot full of tranquilizers.

Ray remained beside the unconscious man long enough to confirm that she'd not killed him, and then, after locating her handbag and making sure that her cellphone was still inside of it, she hightailed it out of the building before the other security guard returned with backup.

Snuffy's exit had created a massive hole in the side of the Quonset hut. Ray raced out through it, and then, knowing she couldn't exit the F-Bio premises any other way, she ran straight ahead, towards the only other available exit: the hole that the departing mammoth had made in the institute's perimeter fence.

Once safely outside of the F-Bio compound, Ray dashed into the woods. It wasn't too long after she'd entered into concealment that she saw several armed men hurry around the side of the institute building and into the Quonset hut she'd just escaped from.

Ray now got her cellphone out of her handbag. She had a phone call to make.

CHAPTER 19

All things being equal, Snuffy would have been unable to break out of his enclosure.

But throw Agent Orange into the mix, and almost any result was possible.

Deep in the woods, Snuffy, the Woolly Mammoth, was assaulted by conflicting emotions and impressions.

The mammoth's first problem was the sheer multitude of unfamiliar smells and sounds he was encountering now that he was outside of his cage.

The smells and sounds confused him. None of them were part of the once-familiar landscape of the steppe-tundra, the frigid plain that had been his home.

In addition to the perplexing odors of unfamiliar fauna, Snuffy also smelled and sensed a multitude of little animals nearby, most of whom cowered in terror when he trampled past them. Those trembling woodland animals could sense that, although Snuffy wasn't a predator, something had gone very wrong with him, and he'd become dangerous in a non-carnivorous but no less terrible way.

The rage that had driven Snuffy to kill Paula was unfamiliar to him, and yet the mammoth had found his feeder's violent death unexpectedly satisfying.

The thrill of that first shedding of human blood was fading. But Snuffy felt the desire to shed more such blood.

But Snuffy's desire to kill was secondary, overshadowed by his desire for something else.

A beacon, a tantalizing smell, summoned him onward.

Like a flavor on Snuffy's tongue, the smell hung in the distant air like sweet spices. It was the same unfamiliar taste that had been in his food tonight, that substance that had started off tasting bitter, but had then turned sweet as honey, and had now developed into a raging craving.

From miles away, Snuffy was smelling the Agent Orange that Stash Harris had stored in his tent.

But it was nighttime, a time when the mammoth usually slept. And Agent Orange, which was what had greatly enhanced Snuffy's sense of smell, now seemed to also add to his diurnal exhaustion.

The result of this was that, as abruptly as if someone had disconnected him from a power source, Snuffy lay down and slept.

And while the corrupted woolly mammoth slept in the woods, and the woodland critters avoided his sleeping bulk in fright, the strange and deadly narcotic that he'd unwittingly eaten worked even more dangerous changes in his body.

CHAPTER 20

The night wore on and morning began.

Over in the F-Bio compound, Dr. Milton Ambrose arrived and reviewed the situation, and preparations were being made to recapture Snuffy.

Over at the Sleepaway Campground, Cherry Soufflé was still partying it up, celebrating what was certain to be their biggest hit ever.

Ray Linn had made her phone calls but hadn't been able to reach the man she desperately needed to contact. She kept on trying, however, until exhaustion claimed her too, and she fell asleep in the woods.

And, in his nice, comfortable bed at home, forest ranger Gary Bentley was dreaming . . .

CHAPTER 21

Gary Bentley dreamt that he was hunting elephants. He was out in the woods, carrying his new Weatherby rifle, and the elephant he was after was eluding him.

It was imperative that he eliminate this particular elephant, which had killed many people.

But so far, no dice. Gary would get the animal in shooting range, and then it would vanish as if by magical means.

And then suddenly, the killer elephant was behind him. It trumpeted loudly, and he spun desperately around and saw it charging at him.

The killer elephant was bright orange in color. Its tusks were orange, too.

But, worst of all, its eyes were also a glowing bright orange.

The elephant's orange eyes were headlights shining beams of insanity into Gary Bentley's mind.

He raised his gun to kill the beast, but the beams of orange light projecting out from its head filled his mind with craziness, and he screamed and screamed in terror.

CHAPTER 22

Gary Bentley shuddered awake with his mind full of terror. It took almost a full minute before the fear left him rational enough to realize that he'd merely had a vivid nightmare.

What the hell!? he thought. *What the damn hell!?*

His wife Charlotte still slept peacefully by his side.

Gary lay there. After a while, he began feeling silly.

It was just a nightmare. Nothing but a nightmare. It's childish for me to feel so damn worried about it.

Careful not to wake Charlotte, Gary sat up in bed and leaned back on a pillow. Then he thought carefully over what he'd dreamt.

Last night's TV program about the revival of dead species clearly affected me more than I thought. And the rest of it? The damn killer elephant was orange in color. That's the easy too: when I met those rockers yesterday, I began worrying that they might have some Agent Orange on them.

And the last element—the Weatherby rifle? That's the easiest one of all. That very same gun is outside in my pickup truck right now!

Having figured all of this out, Gary Bentley prepared to go back to sleep.

Just before he dozed off again, he looked at the wall clock. 4:17 a.m.

CHAPTER 23

A short while after Gary Bentley dozed off again, Ray Linn woke up in the woods, somewhere between the Futures Bioresearch facility and the Lake Placid Trailer Park.

By her wristwatch it was 5 a.m.

Ray got up and stripped off the thermal jumpsuit she'd been wearing, which had prevented from feeling the night's cold while she slept.

She was angry with herself for dozing off, but shrugged it off and immediately dialed her connection again.

The man she was calling was her sort-of boyfriend, Brady Scott. They'd met in a bar a year ago and begun dating after Brady had told her, "Hi, honey, I'm Brady. I'm pansexual. What're your pronouns?"

Brady finally answered the phone.

"Hey, baby, where the hell have you been?"

"Ray? What time is it now? Dammit, baby, couldn't you just wait till sunrise before calling?"

"I called you two hours ago. Voicemail."

"Yeah, sorry. I had a meeting; put my phone on silent; you know what I mean. But, what the hell is so important that it can't wait? Has someone misgendered you again? I've told you time and time again— if you want folks to view you as a woman, stick some silicone in your chest. It never fails."

"Fuck you, Brady, breasts don't make a woman a woman. Now, listen; this is important."

"Listening. Man, this had better be good."

Ray Linn controlled her irritation and gave a short but detailed explanation of everything that had happened to her the previous night.

"For Chrissakes, Ray, what've you been smoking?" Brady groaned after hearing her out. "There's no such things as woolly mammoths anymore."

"There is now. I'll forward the vids to you. Just bring me that fucking chopper and the tranquilizer gun ASAP."

CHAPTER 24

At around the time that Brady Scott was climbing aboard an official UH-1H Iroquois (Huey) helicopter to go pick up Ray Linn, Stash Harris was preparing to go visit his drug connections.

Stash checked his cell phone for the time. It was 6:20 a.m. Then he saw that Henny and Roy Cullens had sent him a text confirming that they'd be at the campground parking lot by 6:30.

Gotta get a move on then, Stash thought.

He pulled on his clothes and sneakers and then opened up his bag. Unlike the others, Stash had a tent all to himself.

Stash got out his Glock 17 automatic from his bag and stuck it in the rear of his belt. Then he turned his attention to the package of Agent Orange.

Hmmm, now how do I handle this?

The drugs in the package belonged to Elkins drug baron Cutthroat Kelly. In this deal Stash was simply the middleman. His role was to hand the goods over and collect a fat wallet of cash in return, which he'd in turn give over to the guys who'd brought the Agent Orange to him.

That part was simple enough. But the problem was that Stash Harris wasn't sure he could trust the buyers.

If I give 'em the drugs and they say they don't have the money, there'll be hell to pay. If they roll me and take the drugs, it's sure to shorten my life. Cutthroat Kelly's likely gonna cut my own throat.

So, what Stash decided was to take just a sample of the Agent Orange to Roy and Henny. Once certain that they were legit, he'd hurry back to the camp and fetch the rest of the stuff for them.

It occurred to Stash that maybe the Cullens were as legit as he was, but it never hurt to be overly cautious.

So, Stash packed up two packages of the twelve in the bag and stuck them in his pants' pockets.

On stepping outside into the dawn, he smiled. Nobody else had woken up yet. Nor did he expect them to, even when he made that return trip. Everyone had partied till 3 a.m. In his experience, no one would be waking up before midmorning.

The ranger's gonna be super pissed-off about all the trash we've scattered everywhere, Stash thought as he walked past the still-smoldering campfire and set off between the trees. *We'd better clean the place up before leaving.*

CHAPTER 25

Gary Bentley had woken up again at about the same time that Stash did.

This second time he'd not dreamt at all. But still, he woke up worried.

Just before he'd opened his eyes this morning, an image had come to his mind: the face of the young man—*Was the kid's name Stash, or what?*—who'd been asked if he'd secured the permits to use the campground as a location for the rock band's video.

Now that Gary remembered that young man, he suddenly had a horrible sense that the 'Curse of Agent Orange' (as he often regarded it nowadays), was about to strike again.

Gary got out of bed and, without bothering to shower, quickly dressed up in his ranger uniform.

His wife Charlotte woke up just as he was lacing up his boots.

"Morning, honey, where are you rushing off to so early?" she asked between yawns.

He bent down and kissed her gently on the lips. "Don't worry about it. Just something I need to check out very quickly."

Charlotte Bentley grinned mischievously. "Okay, honey, but don't you dare shoot any poor bears you happen to run into."

Gary managed to laugh. "Oh, I won't, baby. I'm sure I won't."

Then he rushed out of his house, leapt up into the front of his ranger truck and sped off.

CHAPTER 26

As if the biological 'switch' that had made him fall asleep had been flipped the opposite way, Snuffy woke up with a bang.

The woolly mammoth was immediately angry. The same unfamiliar bloodlust from last night once more addled his brain. He felt an intense desire to harm other animals, but at the moment, there were none nearby.

Snuffy was hungry also, but that hunger was already being replaced by the craving for Agent Orange. Just like he had before falling asleep, Snuffy could smell Stash Harris's far-off packages of Agent Orange.

The animal lumbered up to his feet and followed his nose, with his now bright-orange eyes gleaming like amber traffic lights.

Any trees that stood in Snuffy's way he knocked down to the ground. By now, Agent Orange had doubled the mammoth's strength, making him much more of a force to be reckoned with than nature had originally intended.

The smell of Agent Orange was strong in Snuffy's mind, and it grew even more so as he moved toward the Sleepaway Campground.

***

A short distance along his journey, Snuffy became aware that the smell he was tracking had now split into two separate trails.

Of course, he was now smelling both the large store of Agent Orange that Stash Harris had left in his tent and the two packages of the drug that the man had on his person.

But Snuffy didn't know this. The woolly mammoth simply realized that one of those two trails of addictive scent was closer to him than the other. And that closer trail of scent was getting nearer to him by the second.

And so Snuffy turned aside to investigate that one first.

CHAPTER 27

Stash Harris had been wrong: he wasn't the first person to wake up.

Cherry Soufflé rhythm guitarist Lucian Graves was also wide awake as the sun rose over the autumn mountain landscape.

Lucian had initially woken up to relieve himself. But then, halfway back to the tent, he got caught up in a flash of inspiration.

A rap-rock rhythm had trilled into his brain, and wouldn't depart. Lucian then decided to see it through.

Back in the tent, his girlfriend Vivienne was still passed out cold. He'd pulled a blanket over her, picked up the Takamine acoustic guitar he had lying in the corner, and headed out amongst the trees to follow his muse.

Lucian had walked well away from the camp until he'd crossed the east-west camping trail, and found himself a quiet nook where none of the band would be able to overhear and disturb him.

***

Now, Lucian was busy playing and replaying his new riff, trying to work it into a song:

"Sorry, baby, but you're driven me crazy,
One damn time too many!
Once you were sweeter than wine,
But now, you're makin' me lose my mind
Seems like you always have an axe to grind!"

Hmmm, good, but could be better . . . once I put a fuzz pedal on it, we'll see. The melody's fine, but I'll leave it up to Cherry to come up with better lyrics . . .

Lucian played a little more and then frowned. *Nah, that don't work, I'd better go back to the former version.*

He pulled out his cellphone to record what he'd gotten so far. Then Lucian realized that along with the cellphone he's extracted a small baggie of cocaine.

He smiled at the sight of the coke. "Hell yeah! Now that's more like it."

He spilled some cocaine onto the back of his hand, sniffed it up and looked at the world with clearer vision.

Well, Lucian thought he had clearer vision until he saw the two orange eyes staring back at him through the trees.

"What the fuck?" he gasped in shock, as his eyes took in more and more of the impossible creature peering at him through the trees barely five yards away.

Is that a mammoth? But it can't be, they're extinct.

But either Lucian's cocaine was spiked with acid or the mammoth was real.

And it definitely looked real. An elephant with a shaggy brown coat and those immense yellow tusks but smallish ears.

The mammoth was eating as it watched Lucian, using its trunk to run tree branches through its mouth, and stripping them of whatever foliage they still possessed, which of course, was very little at this time of year.

Lucian could smell the mammoth from where he sat.

So far, the mammoth was just standing there and watching him. Lucian Graves put the rest of his cocaine away, and then did what any modern person in his shoes would: he Googled "Woolly Mammoth" on his cellphone.

"Believed to have finally gone extinct 4,000 years ago," he read aloud.

Lucian got up to his feet and walked towards the mammoth. He felt a little nervous while doing so. He'd just noticed that the front portion of the giant animal's right tusk was stained bright red.

Is that blood on its tusk? How dangerous are these animals anyway? Why are its eyes that bright color? Maybe this isn't such a hot idea.

The closer Lucian got to the mammoth, the more he realized how gigantic it was, the more he considered that he was being dumb by approaching it.

But the cocaine he'd used had made him foolishly brave. Also, he really wanted to make sure that he was seeing what he thought he was seeing. He wanted to make certain he wasn't having some sort of acid flashback or worse.

The mammoth continued stripping branches of their leaves, both its trunk and mouth working much faster now. Lucian sensed that the animal was becoming frustrated with its inability to find the nourishment it sought in what it was eating. He felt almost like he could sense its anger.

Up close, he felt awed by how big it was.

It has to be at least nine feet tall!

He stepped between its tusks and touched its trunk. Yes, the giant animal wasn't a hallucination. To convince himself further, Lucian courageously grabbed on the mammoth's left tusk, the one that wasn't bloody. The ivory was cool as the morning.

Hell yeah! This creature is real. Hey, I know what to do! I'll take some photos and send them to Gideon and the guys and then call everyone and ask them to meet me over here. We can fit this mammoth in our new video!

Lucian Graves stepped back a few paces and snapped away.

But right then, the mammoth stopped eating, leapt toward him, and swiped sideways at him with its immense trunk.

The animal's assault was so unexpected that Lucian had no chance of evading it. He was knocked well off of the ground and flung sideways, flying through the air and finally crashing into a tree.

He'd hit high up the tree trunk and now fell to the ground, where he lay, half stunned.

"What the hell'd you do that for, you overgrown furball," Lucian wheezed in pain. "I was only being friendly."

But there was worse to come for him. Trumpeting like thunder, the mammoth was coming at him again, running toward him with clear bad intent.

Lucian rolled out of its way in the nick of time. It instead hit the tree behind him. The tree trunk split in two vertical halves.

Lucian stared from the tree to the animal, and discovered, to his horror, that it was already attacking him again. This time, the mammoth didn't charge at him. It reared up like a horse and brought both of its front feet down at him. He rolled away again, but the mammoth's feet hit both of his legs.

Lucian screamed bloody murder as he felt his leg bones shatter. The crystal clarity of the agony forced him out of his dazed state.

When he gazed down at his legs, everything from mid-thigh down was completely pulverized, flattened against the forest floor, leaving a bloody mess of pulped muscle and skin and bone splinters.

Lucian Graves screamed again as the mammoth once more reared up. The sheer immensity of its bulk obliterated the forest from his view.

Then it brought down its legs again, this time on Lucian's head, shattering his skull and driving those bloody fragments of skull deep into Lucian's corpse.

CHAPTER 28

"Now, listen up, everybody," Dr. Milton Ambrose was telling the group of men assembled in the front parking lot of the Futures Bioresearch compound. "We need to get this done quickly."

Twelve in number, the doctor's companions were a mixture of scientists and security guards. The security guards all carried tranquilizer guns. The scientists carried boxes of tranquilizer darts to reload the guns.

While speaking, Dr. Ambrose gestured around agitatedly. "It's time to get started; we've wasted enough time waiting for daylight, but we couldn't search the countryside in the dark of night. But we know that our Mammuthus primigenius sleeps at night also. Now, everyone already knows their assignments and their assigned locations, but I'll go over them again." He pointed to three men on his right. "You guys are heading over to the trailer park. Snuffy's unlikely to be over there, but look around—"

"Sir, why can't we just use helicopters to search?" a man interrupted. "We'll cover a hell of a lot more territory that way and a lot faster, too."

"Because we don't want people to know what's going on," Dr. Ambrose replied impatiently. "If we start sweeping the countryside with choppers, folks will soon cotton on to the fact that something's gone wrong out here. Our priority now is to recapture this animal *quietly*, without alerting the public to its existence."

The man who'd asked the question nodded, then said, "Sir, I still can't believe that we had something like that hidden away here all this while."

Dr. Ambrose sighed. "That was the whole point. And now we need to recapture it and hide it away again."

As the men prepared to get into the bus that would drop them off at their assigned search locations, someone asked Dr. Ambrose: "Doc, I really don't like this. Can't we just carry some guns as backup?"

Dr. Ambrose shook his head. "No, and that's final. We don't kill that animal, no matter what happens. It's the only one of its kind in existence. It's way too precious to make extinct again." He frowned at the man who'd posed the question. "And besides, you know the rules: No firearms permitted here—courtesy of you-know-who."

"Yeah, Ms. Pronouns!" said the guard who'd initially discovered Snuffy had escaped.

The other guard, the man that Ray Linn had struck with a rock while making her escape, had been taken to hospital; he had a fractured skull.

Dr. Ambrose frowned. "Listen, guys, I understand your concerns here. You're understandably worried for your safety because our mammoth killed my assistant Paula. But I can assure you that that was entirely an accident. I'm certain that what happened was that Ray Lin provoked the animal and once she'd goaded it up sufficiently, she then pushed our dear Paula into its way. And her/his whole aim in getting Paula killed would be to shut down this research facility for unsafe practices and make all of us—myself included—lose our jobs. You know what that *person* is like."

The men nodded angrily at this.

"So, let's go find our poor mammoth," Dr. Ambrose finished up. "We'll have the police arrest Ray Linn later."

Dr. Ambrose and his men climbed into their bus and set off on their search.

***

Dr. Ambrose was understandably furious at Snuffy's escape.

The climax of a lifetime's work—my shot at snaring the Nobel Prize . . . about to be ruined by . . . I can't believe that woke asshole could be so vindictive! Once we get out of this mess, I'm going to ensure that she's prosecuted. I don't give a damn if her/his father is the US President! We can throw her/him in jail for breaking in here and assaulting Jose. Thank God that she didn't kill him!

But Dr. Ambrose was also worried.

He prayed that he was right about his escaped wooly mammoth being harmless. Yes, Paula's death he could explain away as Ray Linn's fault. But he prayed that Snuffy wasn't currently causing any serious harm or damage to life or property that might help Ray Lin close F-Bio down for good.

CHAPTER 29

Roy and Henny Cullens were waiting for Stash when he arrived at the campground parking lot.

The Cullens were standing beside their ride, a blue Nissan sedan with a cute teardrop camper trailer hitched to it. The husband was tall and thin, and the wife was short and fat. Both of them were middle-aged and looked nondescript, not the sort of people you'd normally associate with the sale of narcotics.

Stash distrusted both husband and wife on sight. He'd not met them before; the deal for the Agent Orange had been set up by Cutthroat Kelly and the Cullens' boss, whom Stash didn't know. But Stash was naturally suspicious.

"You're late," Roy Cullen told Stash when he reached them.

"What's it matter, so long as the dope's on time?" Stash retorted.

"Yeah, I guess so," Roy Cullen replied.

"He's pissed 'cos he thought you were gonna stand us up," Henny explained.

Next, Roy Cullen looked Stash over from top to bottom. "You got the goods on you, man? Cuz you don't look like you're carrying a hundred G's worth of anything."

Stash smirked. "I got enough orange on me to prove I'm legit. Once I see the money and confirm you're legit too, you'll get the rest of it."

"Hey, what is this shit?" Roy Cullen asked.

Stash almost expected him to go for a gun then, because he was certain the man had one on him. But then he smiled.

Nah. His wife is the one packing. That's why she ain't standing right next to him, so I won't see her if she pulls heat on me.

"Like I said," Stash said. "You'll get the dope when I see the money's right here."

"That ain't what we were told," Henny said. "You were supposed to meet us here with everything."

Stash laughed now. "Yeah, that's what my boss told me too. But let's just say, I've been dealing for so long that I've got major trust issues where shit like this is concerned." He gestured at Roy Cullens. "For instance, how do I know you two are even who claim to be? Huh? You could've bumped the real Roy and Henny Cullens off and switched places with 'em."

"You're fucking paranoid," Roy said, with a look of amazement on his face. "Of course, we're who we say we are!"

"Humor me then," Stash smiled back. "This is the drug biz. Everyone's paranoid."

Henny rolled her eyes. "Okay, okay. Let's get this over with."

After looking around him to ensure no one was watching their transaction, Stash pulled a transparent package of Agent Orange out of his pocket and handed it to Roy. "I've got one more of these on me here and ten more back in the woods," he told Roy as the man peeled back the sell-o-tape the package had been sealed with.

"Hold on. Let me taste it to make sure it's the real thing."

Roy pulled out one of the little orange 'candies' and licked it. Then he spat out the taste and nodded at his wife. "Yeah, baby, it's the real deal."

Henny Cullens had seemed tense all of this while, but now Stash saw her shoulders sag in relief.

He smiled at them both. "So, I don't rip you guys off, you don't rip me off and we'll be the best of friends for life."

Roy put the chunk of Agent Orange back in the package, sealed it up again, and handed it back to Stash.

Then Roy frowned. "You know, man, I've been in this drug racket since I was a teenager. I've shot folk over drugs, been shot myself and even done a spell in the penitentiary for trafficking in narcotics.

In all of that fucking time, I've experienced people at their goddamn worst—like drug addiction literally brings out the worst in people."

He paused and looked at Stash for confirmation of this. Stash nodded and he went on:

". . . Yeah, all of that time, I've seen women kill their own babies for a fix, and once in the house I lived in, a teenager chopped up his own parents with an axe for fix money. I've watched women copulate with animals simply to earn money to buy junk or meth . . . I've seen people literally shit themselves to death because the fix was bad. I've seen junkies overdose on shit and they were smiling as they died, like they could see God welcoming them into heaven. But . . ."

Roy Cullens stared down at the package of orange 'marshmallows' that he'd just handed back to Stash and seemed unable to continue speaking.

Stash knew what he wanted to say, and he said it for him:

"But in all of that damn time, man, you've never seen a drug that makes addicts act the way Agent Orange does, right?"

Roy Cullens nodded. "Yeah, man, that's right."

"It's like Agent Orange taps into the most primitive area of the human brain and makes it override our reasoning faculties," Henny Cullens said.

"Yeah, you look into those addicts' eyes, and it's almost like they've become possessed," Roy said.

Henny nodded. "Yeah, Roy and I don't want nothing to do with that. But we were coming this way, and so we got the call to make the buy."

Stash nodded. He felt a sudden weight on his conscience. Like here was this damn killer drug that literally turned people into psychopaths, and he was helping sell it.

"Hey, I'm only the middleman too," he clarified to the Cullens with hands raised in a gesture of innocence. "I wouldn't touch this stuff either if it weren't that one doesn't refuse instructions from Cutthroat Kelly. He ain't called 'Cutthroat' for no reason."

Roy Cullens laughed at that.

"Hey, you're alright, man," he told Stash and slapped him on the back. "Come on in the camper and I'll show you the money, then you get us the rest of the drugs and we'll all be done with this deal. Hopefully, next time we meet up, we'll be dealing just weed and coke."

Leaving Henny outside to watch, Stash and Roy climbed into the teardrop camper.

Roy got out a thin attaché case and opened it up. The case was piled with stacks of used bills: hundreds, fifties, and twenties held in bundles by rubber bands.

After a perfunctory count, Stash nodded to Roy.

"Cool, I'll go get you the rest of the stuff."

He and Roy stepped out again and found Henny looking confused, she was staring at the trees across the from the parking lot, by the road that led out of the campground.

"What's the matter, hon?" Roy asked.

"I dunno," Henny said. "But since you guys went in the camper, I've had the feeling of someone watching me. Watching us all, in fact."

Roy shot Stash a worried look. "Are you expecting company?"

Stash shook his head. "I'm here with a rock band, but we all partied hard last night and everyone's still asleep."

"Look!" Henny said, pointing. "Is that an elephant?"

"Huh?" Stash and her husband exclaimed together, with Roy adding, "An elephant in West Virginia?"

But whatever it was, it was heading for them. The trees were thick at that point and their leaves were a golden brown. And what was approaching through them was also brownish in color.

"That's not an elephant," Stash told Roy. "It's a mammoth."

"It can't be a mammoth," Roy replied. "Those are extinct."

"It's a mammoth," Stash replied as the huge animal broke out through the tree cover and headed for them.

"Stop arguing, both of you!" Henny shrieked at them both. "Look at that goddamn animal's eyes! I don't know how it's possible, but it looks like its addicted to Agent Orange!"

Both men gaped at the mammoth and realized that what Henny had said was true. Both of them instantly recognized the telltale bright orange eyes.

"Fuck, It's a crackhead elephant!" Roy said in alarm.

"No, a crackhead mammoth!" Stash told him. "A crack-mammoth!"

"Are you both nuts?!?" Henny screamed at them both as the mammoth got nearer and nearer to them. "Who cares which it is!? Fucking run for your damn lives! That thing is covered in blood! It's clearly dangerous!"

As if it agreed with her assessment, the mammoth trumpeted loudly and fiercely at them. It left no mistake in their minds that it had targeted them for attack.

Stash, Roy, and Henny turned and ran across the parking lot for the shelter of the woods. They looked back, saw the giant animal coming after them, and kept right on going.

Henny had gotten a head start on the two men, but all of a sudden she tripped and fell over.

Her husband stopped running to help her up. "Shit, honey, get up, get up!' he shouted, while Henny seemed frozen down there on the ground. Her mouth agape in terror, she could only tremble and moan as the mammoth reached the two of them.

Stash hadn't stopped running. He kept running until he reached the trees and then turned to see what was going to happen.

***

The charging mammoth reached the Cullens and came to an abrupt halt. Stash thought that if it had been a car, its tires would have screeched in loud protests.

86

For a moment, nothing happened. The moment extended on and Stash was beginning to think that they'd merely imagined and exaggerated the danger—

Because, let's face it, a crackhead mammoth? C'mon, man, how the hell's that even possible?

—But then the mammoth moved again.

The mammoth suddenly raised its foot and stomped on Henny.

She screamed.

Stash wasn't so far off that he couldn't see what had happened. The mammoth had stomped its foot all the way through Henny's body. Its massive leg looked like a tree trunk growing up through Henny's belly. Henny squirmed around the impalement like a bug on a pin and began vomiting blood while yet more blood squirted out from her insides around the mammoth's toes.

At first Roy Cullens seemed frozen by the shock of what had just happened. But then, his mind thawed and he turned and ran.

Or rather, he tried to run. Before he'd taken his third step, the mammoth had snared him around the neck with its trunk and dragged him back towards it.

Stash winced as the mammoth swung Roy Cullen up into the sky like he was a Ken doll. Roy went up, up, up, till he seemed very small; and then he came down again, gradually increasing in size. Roy had gone up screaming in shock, and he came down again screaming in terror at his inevitable crash to death on the concrete parking lot.

He's gonna get pulped! Stash thought. What he was witnessing had the elements of a dream, or as if he was getting high from marijuana, he'd not yet smoked.

However, seemingly by some serious bad fortune, Roy Cullens ended up landing right on the back of the rampaging mammoth.

Stash winced at the impact. He thought he heard some of Roy's bones shattering as he crash-landed. Possibly, that horrible crunch had been the sound of his spine being uncoupled.

Roy lay there on the mammoth's back, unmoving.

The mammoth seemed to be waiting for him to fall off. When this didn't happen, it reared up like a horse, and Roy came rolling down.

Yes, now there was no doubt in Stash's mind. The horrible crash-landing *had* broken Roy's back. He landed on the ground in a misarranged heap. His arms and legs twitched, but there seemed to be no conscious coordination in the movement of his digits. Blood streamed from his mouth.

Henny was long dead by now. Roy reached out a hand toward her corpse as the mammoth began stomping on him too.

***

Stash had thought he was safely hidden away in the trees, but then, once the killer mammoth got through stomping Roy Cullens to paste, it began sniffing the air.

Finally, it turned its attention directly towards Stash Harris.

There was no mistaking this. Stash knew that the mammoth was staring directly at him.

The animal began moving slowly in his direction. Its front feet were drenched in blood and each step it took left bloody foot marks on the parking lot.

If I run, it'll run after me, Stash thought desperately. *And I can't lead it back to the campsite; it'll kill everyone there.*

Figuring that the only safe direction was up, Stash grabbed hold of a low-hanging branch and began climbing a tree.

The mammoth reached the tree and stopped. It looked up at Stash and Stash looked down at it.

Terror had given Stash the sort of climbing agility that his high school gym coach had wished he'd had. Back then, Stash had been crap on the climbing ropes.

Now, however, he'd scaled the tree like an ape and was high, high up its branches, too high for the mammoth to reach him even when it reared on its rear legs and extended its trunk up at him.

It didn't occur to Stash Harris that the mammoth was after the Agent Orange in his pockets and that he could possibly deflect its attention away from himself by throwing the pair of packages in his pockets down to the beast.

The mammoth trumpeted up at him as if ordering him to throw the drugs down, or else . . . But Stash was far off in a realm of panic, and any sort of interspecies communication wasn't working for him.

What did occur to Stash was to shoot the mammoth.

This was logical enough. The mammoth's head was very close to him.

It'll be impossible for me to miss a shot from this close range. Big as it is, a bullet in one of its eyes should likely scramble its unhinged brain and kill it.

But when Stash reached back into his waistband for his Glock, he discovered it was gone. He'd lost it somewhere along the mad dash for his life.

Shit! he thought in disappointment.

But the mammoth was already moving away from the tree.

Huh, it's leaving? Stash wondered in relief, not believing his luck, as a few yards away lay the bloody mess that a short while ago had been Roy and Henny Cullens.

But Stash's relief was short-lived. Suddenly, the retreating mammoth turned around again and charged at Stash's tree.

The impact with which it hit the tree almost dislodged Stash from the branch on which he was perched. But Stash clung on for dear life and managed not to fall the fifteen feet or so to the forest floor.

The mammoth trumpeted up at Stash one more time, then retreated and repeated the maneuver.

This time, Stash Harris wasn't so lucky. The tree didn't topple over when the mammoth hit it, but it shook so violently that when the branch Stash was sitting on snapped back into position, it catapulted Stash out into the air over the parking lot.

Just like Roy Cullens, Slash went high up and then came down again, with his body flailing wildly as he came down to that inevitably disastrous meeting with the concrete flooring.

Yelling in horror, Stash hit the parking lot head-first. His head burst open like someone had detonated TNT inside of it.

CHAPTER 30

While Stash Harris' body twitched its life away and his blood squirted out from his exploded head, Snuffy the Mammoth dug his trunk into Stash's pockets and extracted the two packages of Agent Orange they contained.

The mammoth swallowed both packages, and while his digestive system separated plastic from narcotic, he lumbered off across the parking lot towards the woods, making his way towards that second, much larger batch of Agent Orange.

Killing the three humans had been a very satisfying activity. And Snuffy could smell that there were lots more humans where he was headed.

His brain now overrun by Agent Orange, Snuffy felt a deep psychotic joy. Killing those humans also would be just as satisfying.

CHAPTER 31

If Dr. Ambrose was concerned about keeping his search for Snuffy quiet and low-key, Ray Linn wasn't.

Ray gestured impatiently at the white and blue Huey helicopter as it circled and then dropped lower in the sky.

She nodded in satisfaction when she saw that, as she'd instructed him to, her boyfriend Brady Scott had come alone.

The chopper landed, but Brady, who was piloting it, kept the rotors spinning.

Ray ducked under the loudly whirling propellers and climbed up into the front of the helicopter. She leaned over and kissed Brady, and then buckled herself into her seat.

"Hey, baby, you finally made it," she told him.

"The trank gun and darts are behind your seat," Brady shouted over the noise of the engines as he took the chopper back up again. "But, Ray, honey, why the hell don't you want us involving HQ? We'll find the escaped mammoth much faster if we get more searchers."

Ray shook her head emphatically. "Involving too many people will ruin our chances at being promoted," she replied. "We don't wanna share the credit for this with anyone else."

Brady smirked coldly at the cold wisdom in her words. "True, true." Then he asked. "Which way are we headed?"

Ray pointed east. "That way, towards the Sleepaway Campground."

Brady nodded and turned their helicopter in that direction.

CHAPTER 32

The other member of the Cherry Soufflé entourage who was up early in the woods that morning was video director Gideon Thorne. But while the band's (now deceased) rhythm guitarist Lucian Graves had been carried off into the woods by a burst of musical inspiration, Gideon was out among the trees attending to a more basic call of nature.

The man was taking a shit.

Gideon Thorne had reservations about shitting in the woods. It was so inconvenient. You're crouched down over the grass, leaving your ass as a target for snakes.

And as luck would have it, so far, I'm the only one who's had to go! Everyone else is snoring away in their sleeping bags and I've got the runs.

But at least he wasn't having to use leaves to wipe his backside. He had more than enough toilet paper.

Aside from his tummy troubles, Gideon was in a great mood:

Yeah, this is the video that'll make my career. After this, I'll be strictly A-list material.

Gideon was just about to wipe his ass clean when he smelled something nearby. In fact, it smelled like really bad shit.

What the heck? Why does my crap stink so bad all of a sudden?

But then he realized that the intensified smell wasn't coming from below him, but from above him.

Gideon Thorne looked up and then yowled in dismay. A massive anus was opening up over him.

Gideon was helpless as the inexplicable anus drenched him with feces.

Gideon was naturally incensed at being shat on. Who wouldn't be? But once he straightened up and saw exactly what had shat on him, his anger fled away from him like a scared bird.

Gideon Thorne fainted. Unfortunately for him, he fell right back into the massive mound of mammoth dung.

CHAPTER 33

Gary Bentley pulled up his pickup truck into the Sleepaway Campground parking lot and leapt down.

He'd parked first in a line of vehicles. Two other vehicles were parked opposite those.

It seemed odd to Gary that there were so many cars here on a Tuesday, but then he remembered yesterday's rock band.

Oh, so Cherry Soufflé didn't go home last night.

Maybe it was a kind of intuition from doing this same job for so long, but Gary was already getting a bad vibe from being here this morning. He felt agitated without really understanding why.

Once he walked out from between his ranger truck and the blue Nissan with the cute teardrop camper trailer hitched to it, he saw the man lying down on the parking lot.

Actually, Gary only saw the man's booted feet. The view of the rest of his body was obstructed by a car.

He hurried over to the car and looked.

Oh, shit.

The man's head was fragmented, literally split into front and rear halves, and his brains were on the ground a few yards away from him.

Gary stared at the corpse in horror. *How the hell did this happen? This guy clearly had an accident of some kind. But unless—Gary squinted skyward, up into the cloudy blue—yeah, unless he fell from up there, how's he gonna burst his head open like this?*

Then Gary looked properly at the dead man's face and recognized him.

Hey, this is the guy that the band called Stash! But what the hell killed him like this?

Before Gary could begin to answer that question, something else caught his attention. He saw a small orange nugget, down by the corpse's leg.

Gary Bentley sighed in dismay and bent down to pick up the candy-like orange chunk.

Not willing to believe his bad luck, he raised the orange chunk to his lips and licked it.

Oh, shit, no! IT IS orange!

He stuck the chunk in his pocket and studied the dead man some more, trying to make sense of what was going on here.

Okay, so this guy Stash was dealing 'orange.' But if he was selling it, who was buying it? Are they here also?

This was when Gary Bentley really looked around the parking lot and finally noticed the weird mess on his left, over near the edge of the forest.

From a distance, the mess on the concrete made no sense to Gary. It was mostly a wide smear, like someone had dumped oil on the parking lot. It had some large bumps in it, but it was mostly just that broad smear.

Gary walked over to investigate it. And when he realized what he was staring at, he began running.

He reached the mess, got a good look at the two pulped corpses and threw up on them. He couldn't help himself.

Afterwards he wiped his lips clean and resumed trying to make sense of what he was looking at. He could see that the mess was comprised of two bodies, a man's and a woman's, but how they'd both become so flattened, Gary couldn't even start to conjecture.

He managed to resist the urge to throw up again and then paid more attention to his surroundings.

He noticed the blood marks on the ground.

Are those footprints? But what kind of animal makes footprints like that, so big and almost circular?

While thinking this, Gary began walking quickly back towards his ranger truck. He was glad he'd not yet removed the Weatherby Mark V rifle from the truck.

And then, right as Gary reached his truck and was opening up its rear door, he heard a loud trumpeting sound. Then he heard that same sound again.

That's an elephant noise! Huh? An elephant? Here in these West Virginian woods?

Hesitantly, his mind connected the dots. *First, I've got two completely flattened corpses. Second, I've got a guy whose head's been burst open like he fell from the sky or something. And thirdly, I've got massive bloody footprints, like Godzilla's been tramping around in the campground parking lot.* He sighed miserably. *Oh yeah, and last, but definitely not least, I've got Agent Orange. Agent Orange—the gift that keeps on giving . . . me ulcers.*

Dear God, no!

Gary debated on calling for backup. The problem he now faced was his own doubt that he hadn't simply imagined hearing that elephant noise.

Yep, I'm certain I heard it. But I know too, that I dreamt about a rampaging orange killer elephant last night. And that might be influencing me, making me hear and see what I wanna hear. I need to make sure my dreams aren't affecting my professional judgment.

He looked over at the three corpses. *They'll keep for now. It ain't like calling the paramedics is gonna do them any—*

Gary stopped thinking when he saw a huge shape moving deep in the woods. Something gigantic had definitely been there between the trees. Then he blinked and it seemingly wasn't there anymore.

Gary couldn't even say just what he'd seen. But this was autumn, and where the trees were thinly populated, like over where he'd seen whatever it had been, visibility was really good.

Gary grabbed hold of his Weatherby hunting rifle. He knew the gun was loaded, so he didn't bother to check on that.

Then he slammed the truck door shut and ran across the parking lot into the woods.

CHAPTER 34

Once he was inside the woods, he found the mammoth's trail easy to follow.

I just gotta follow all of these huge sunken footprints and the markers of dislodged trees!

Despite the horror that he was leaving behind him, Gary Bentley's first encounter in the woods was a comic one.

Announced by a stink that he'd only ever smelled before in a zoo, Gary suddenly almost bumped into a man who was covered head to toe in animal dung.

Gary stared at him in shock. The dung-covered man looked and smelled so revolting that Gary instinctively pointed his rifle at him, as if warn him to stay back.

"Who're you?" he demanded. "What the hell happened to you?"

"Hi, ranger," the man greeted him. "It's me, Gideon Thorne. You know, the video director from yesterday?"

Gary nodded in disbelief, and the man went on:

"As for why I look like this now? It's something out of a sci-fi novel. I was taking a shit and then I got shit on by a giant woolly mammoth. Do you believe that, sir? A giant wooly mammoth with glowing orange eyes."

Gary looked at Gideon in horror as the dots continued to connect in his mind. "Did you say a *woolly mammoth* did this? Those are extinct, you know."

Gideon Thorne laughed. "Yeah, ranger, I know, right? Man, even those *Sharknado* Asylum guys couldn't dream shit like this up."

"Come with me quick," Gary told him. "We've gotta get to your campsite."

But Gideon Thorne firmly shook his head in refusal. "Hell no, sir. I am going to soak myself in the river over there. That's the only way, I'll ever smell normal again."

Gary couldn't argue with that. He watched the totally befouled Gideon Thorne hurry towards the river. And then he hurried after his 'elephant' prey again, once more following the deep impressions left by its giant feet.

His mind felt like it was coming loose at the seams.

A mammoth? I'm dealing with a killer mammoth that's addicted to Agent Orange?

CHAPTER 35

While the park ranger was addressing the stinky video director, the killer mammoth had already arrived at the campsite.

The campsite was still peaceful and quiet, with no signs of life except for the noise of two copulating couples.

Snuffy sniffed the air again and quickly located the drug he was after. The Agent Orange was in the last tent across the campsite, the small one set slightly off from the others; the one that reeked with the smell of the man who'd been up in the tree near that wide open space.

All Snuffy had to do to reach this tent was walk around the others, straight through the extinguished campfire.

However, by this point, killing humans had become another form of addiction for Snuffy, second only to his craving for Agent Orange.

And so, to satiate his bloodlust, Snuffy took the longer, more scenic route to his drugs. He trampled his way through both of the intervening tents on that side of the campfire pit.

Two of Snuffy's first victims were a couple having sex. Once he'd stepped on them, shattering their backs, their dying screams immediately woke up most of the others in the tents.

In the confusion that now ensued, a few people got their wits about them in time to save their lives, but most were killed by Snuffy while they were still trying to work out what was going.

The two tents crashed down on the dead and the dying, and the latter tent then got tangled up with the mammoth and was dragged along by him, so that when the campers in the single long tent on the opposite side of the campfire emerged through its entrance, they, at first, had no idea what had flattened almost everyone on the other side of the forest clearing.

All that they saw was a massacre, dead and dying half-pulped people with shattered limbs and exposed bones, moaning and screaming, and rolling about if they still could.

As to what had done this to their friends and lovers, all that the fortunate survivors could initially make out was that one of the tents opposite theirs seemed to have come alive and was now violently attacking Stash's tent.

"We're not really seeing this, are we?" lead guitarist Damien Blackwood asked, while smothering a yawn.

His girlfriend, lead singer Cherry Angel, nodded. "No, we're not, baby. That dickhead Stash must've mixed LSD into our pot last night."

"Yeah," someone else agreed. "Cuz I ain't never seen a tent with hairy legs and a tail before."

"But if we're hallucinating this, why does the blood and gore look so real?" someone asked.

But then, background vocalist Elara Nightshade ran past them, butt naked and carrying just her cellphone. "Somebody help! A hairy elephant is murdering everyone! Help!"

Still screaming, she vanished into the woods.

Cherry Angel, her boyfriend Damien Blackwood, and everyone else who'd come out of the tent to stare at the absurd nightmare opposite them, looked at each other in astonishment.

"A hairy elephant?" someone asked in confusion.

And that was when the 'hairy elephant' in question shook off the tent that had fallen over it, and they could properly see what it was.

"What the hell is that thing?" Cherry Angel asked, pointing over at the woolly mammoth with a trembling hand.

Her boyfriend shook his head. "No, baby! We all know what the hell it is. But what the fuck is it doing here, killing people?"

"Yeah," a third person agreed, then asked in turn: "And why the hell is it ransacking its way through Stash's tent like that, turning everything upside down?"

CHAPTER 36

Ray Linn and Brady Scott's helicopter was hovering over the eastern end of the campground, the portion out near Lake Placid and farthest from the parking lot.

"Do you see anything down there?" Brady shouted to Ray who was leaning out of the chopper and looking down into the woods.

Ray leaned back inside and shook her head. "Nothing."

"I'll fly us in closer to the camp then."

Ray nodded. "Do it slowly. Even though the damn mammoth is so big and should therefore be easy to spot, and the trees have hardly any leaves left, we might still miss it if we go too fast."

Brady nodded. "Yeah, babe, but there's also a lot of ground for us to cover. I'll take the chopper down lower so you can see better."

"Yes, do that," Ray Linn agreed.

Leaning back out of the helicopter again, she resumed studying the open patches of green forest floor between the red, gold, and brown crowns of the trees.

After a while of additional fruitless searching, Ray leaned back in again.

"You saw that fucking mammoth," she told Brady angrily, "It's as big as a house. How the hell can it seemingly vanish in the woods?"

"Patience, dude, we'll find it," Brady shouted back at her, then grimaced when he realized his gendering mistake.

But for once, Ray Linn was too distracted to notice that she'd been misgendered.

CHAPTER 37

"Hello, this is 9-1-1. What is your emergency?"

"I'm in the w-w-woods ca-camping with friends and an-an-an elephant—a giant hairy-hairy elephant ran into our tent and began killing everyone," Elara Nightshade told the woman at the other end.

"What that's you just said, ma'am?" the 9-1-1 operator asked in a confused voice. "A giant hairy elephant attacked you and your friends?"

"Yeah, yeah. It was like one of those prehistoric hairy elephants."

"Ma'am are you saying a 'mammoth' attacked you in the woods? Are you serious, or is this a prank call?"

"I'm fucking serious. The eleph—okay, yeah ma-mammoth is ransacking our camp now. I can see it through the trees! It killed my boyfriend!"

"Where are you exactly, ma'am?"

"I'm at the Sleepaway Campground. My name is Elara Nightshade. I'm a singer in the rock band Cherry Soufflé."

"Okay, you're in a rock band, and a woolly mammoth is now killing your friends. Ma'am, have you been doing drugs?"

Elara Nightshade stared at her cell phone in anger. "Yes, I have been doing lots of drugs!" she replied to the operator in a hysterical voice. "And no, those drugs aren't at the moment responsible for what I am seeing. There really is a fucking mammoth here at the fucking campground and it's fucking killing people!"

"Okay, I see, ma'am."

Elara's phone clicked dead. She gaped at it in horror.

"What the hell?" she asked herself, then ducked behind a tree when the deadly animal suddenly looked in her direction.

CHAPTER 38

Snuffy finally located the Agent Orange in Stash's tent.

Snuffy ripped the bag of drugs open with his tusks and began transferring the packages of Agent Orange that it contained up to his mouth.

With each swallow, a fresh thrill of insanity coursed through the mammoth's veins, a fresh rush of nebulous rage that could only calmed by the sight of red blood flowing from damaged flesh.

Impatient to get to work on the nearby humans who were still struggling to come to terms with what was going on, Snuffy quickly finished the drugs and then turned to face them.

By now, several people had crossed the campfire and were staring down at the dead people in horror.

"Oh my God!" someone wept. "Oh, my dear God!"

At least three people had ducked back into the tent to grab their cellphones. Two of these were female vloggers who wanted to upload the carnage to their YouTube and Instagram accounts.

The sole person who intended to call for help couldn't find his cell phone anywhere.

And anyway, it was too late to call for help now.

With his murderous rage revitalized and his eyes flashing like tiny gemstones, Snuffy lowered his head and charged at the closest humans.

The first to suffer was the guy who couldn't find his cell phone. He was immediately spitted on one of Snuffy's immense tusks.

Once he began howling in agony, everyone else ran for safety.

CHAPTER 39

Gary Bentley arrived at Cherry Soufflé's campsite just as Snuffy was flinging the impaled man off of his tusk. The man sailed away through the air like a Frisbee. Gary watched the arc of the man's rise and descent and saw him crash into the river. He watched a moment longer till the man resurfaced, floating on his belly in a widening pool of red.

Gary returned his attention to the foreground. Despite the high-caliber firearm in his hands, for the moment, he felt powerless to act. Gary felt paralyzed with shock, entranced with horror at the vista of human carnage that faced him here.

Watching the flattened people, the bloody corpses, and the impossible animal at the center of it all was like staring at a deranged painting come to life.

The mammoth itself seemed to defy description. It was huger than Gary would have thought from the artist recreations and movie mammoths he'd seen. Those had nothing on this beast. He was certain that the Agent Orange the animal had consumed had contributed to its excessive size.

Unlike in several previous cases of animal addiction to Agent Orange that Gary had witnessed, the mammoth seemed mostly unaltered from its basic furball shape; it had no horny coating of body armor or sharp claws or sharp teeth. Or maybe, if its body was armored now, the horny plates were concealed by its thick coat of maroon-colored hair.

But what it lacked in offensive/defensive modifications, it clearly made up for in size. Gary looked at its legs. Thick as tree trunks themselves, all four were splattered with blood up to the knees, with

106

the front pair splattered higher than that. The mammoth's head was also covered in blood, as were its ears, which though much smaller than an elephant's, nonetheless seemed to flap with a life of their own when it trumpeted its rage at the sky.

But worst of all was the mammoth's bright orange eyes. Eyes that glittered like stars; eyes that shone like the sun; eyes that promised deranged bloody murder to one and all.

Gary now remembered that he was carrying a gun. He looked down at the Weatherby Mark V, looked back up at the humongous animal he needed to kill with the weapon, and then looked down at the gun again.

This damn thing is supposed to be an elephant gun. I sure hope it lives up to that designation, cuz lives are at stake here.

The woolly mammoth already had a second victim. It had its trunk wrapped around the heels of this young woman, one of the vloggers, and was whirling her about around its head, while she shrieked like a whistle fed through a Doppler effect.

The mammoth didn't let go of her either, but instead smashed her down on a tree. This in itself should have killed her, and it appeared to have done so, but the crazy scenario wasn't over even now.

The rampaging mammoth apparently wanted to whirl the girl around some more and so it tugged on her feet to get her out of the tree, but, either her head had gotten stuck in the crook between two branches, or her hair had gotten entwined in them and it couldn't shake her free.

The mammoth dragged her feet and she stretched out like she was on a rack. She wasn't dead either, as her fresh bout of screaming revealed. But then her neck extended past the point of no return and Gary heard its vertebrae snap apart, and suddenly this unfortunate young woman looked something like a human giraffe.

The mammoth tired of her then, and let go of her feet. She slumped down, her head in the tree, her body on the ground, her neck like the ladder one would descend to get from one to the other.

Gary raised his gun and did some quick thinking:

The sole reason this monster came here is because that guy Stash apparently had more Agent Orange here! The damn fool has gotten all of his friends killed!

The mammoth was already ransacking the other tent in search of fresh victims. The tent's front pegs had been wrenched out of the ground and the tent swung lopsidedly from side to side, like it would collapse at any moment.

And from the sound of screaming coming from the interior of the tent, the killer animal had just found someone new to torment and kill.

Gary took careful aim at the mammoth with the Weatherby Mark V . . .

CHAPTER 40

. . . And missed.

Gary Bentley didn't miss hitting the mammoth because he was a bad shot. Far from it.

He missed because right at the moment when he began squeezing the trigger of the hunting rifle, a naked young woman ran towards him.

Gary managed to jerk the barrel of the rifle upwards just in time, or else he'd have blown her brains out. He was relieved to see the shot go over her head, up into the trees.

"Hey, watch it, wilya, missy!" he gasped.

She, however grabbed onto him. "Listen, ranger, you've gotta call the cops! I called them, but they didn't believe me. They thought I was stoned! You've gotta call them! They'll listen to you!"

"Maybe, they will, but I ain't got the time at the moment," Gary told her. "Now get behind me. I gotta shoot this damn killer animal dead."

The mammoth had withdrawn from the tent, and was holding up a young man. Its trunk was wrapped around the throat of the young man who was choking to death.

Gary worked the bolt of the rifle, and chambered a fresh cartridge. Then he took careful aim at the mammoth again.

Okay, I can still save this guy! But I gotta put a bullet in the animal's head and hope it doesn't fall on him when it goes down.

But this time, when Gary fired, the mammoth reared up suddenly and Gary shot its victim instead.

The mammoth turned his head this way and that, seemingly wondering why his plaything was leaking blood from his chest when it hadn't gored him yet.

Shit! Gary worked the bolt again, and again took careful aim.

And then he was once more forced to fire wide when Cherry Angel and Damien Blackwood ran right at him.

"Dammit, are all of you rockers this suicidal?" Gary growled at the pair after this second diverted bullet had zinged harmlessly off into the treetops. "At this rate I'll run out of ammo before I put this thing down!"

"Sorry, sir!" Cherry Angel said.

"Yeah, man, something is seriously wrong with that animal," her boyfriend added.

As if sensing it was under attack, the mammoth flung the wounded man to the ground. Then it stomped on his head.

Everyone winced as the guy's head collapsed flat and streams of pulped brain squirted out from the cracks in it.

With just about everyone in the immediate vicinity dead, the woolly mammoth now turned its attention in their direction.

"Shit, it's looking right at us!" Elara Nightshade shrieked at them all. "What are we gonna do!?"

"Whatever it is that you do, just don't get in front of me again. I gotta make every shot count now."

He took aim again and fired.

This time he hit the animal, but not critically. It had lowered its head to charge at them and he only got it in the shoulder. The impact of the bullet didn't so much as make it stagger, but it shrieked in pain, and charged at Gary and his companions.

It was already quite close to them and it came on as unstoppably as a derailed freight train.

"Go, go, go!" Gary shrieked and leapt sideways, just before the rampaging angry animal crashed through the trees they'd been hiding behind.

***

Miraculously, no one was hurt this time; the furious mammoth missed them all. Avoiding the noise that the mammoth was making as it crashed through the woods looking for them, Gary and his three companions—Elara Nightshade, Cherry Angel, and Damien Blackwood, circled the camp to a point that Gary thought was safe.

"Listen," he told the others. "The worst thing we can do now is make a run for the parking lot. That mammoth is a lot faster than us and it'll kill us all before we can make it there."

"We need to call for help!" Elara told Gary.

"Neither Cherry nor I have our cellphones," Damien told her. "Why haven't *you* called for help?"

Elara replied with tears in her eyes: "*I did.* The woman asked me if I'd been doing drugs. I got mad and said yes, and she hung up on me!"

After pondering the irony that Cherry Angel and Damien Blackwood, who were both dressed, had no cellphone on them, and Elara Nightshade, who was butt-naked, *was* clutching a cellphone, Gary told the three musicians: "Hold on, while I get my cellphone out and call for help." He sighed. "I was gonna do so earlier, and then they'd have arrived here by now. But it would be too late to save your friends anyhow."

He looked cautiously around, made certain that the killer mammoth wasn't in sight, and then handed his gun to Damien to hold for him.

Gary got out his cellphone and dialed.

"Hello, this is 9-1-1. What is your emergency?" the dispatcher asked.

"I'm forest ranger Gary Bentley, and I've got a bad situation here at—"

Gary stopped speaking because he'd seen something out of the corner of his right eye. He turned and saw that the mammoth was

111

watching them from barely ten yards away, and was lowering its head to charge at them.

How the hell did the animal sneak up on us without us hearing it!?

The mammoth charged at them.

"Get out of the way!" Gary yelled at the musicians and then dove to the left.

No one except Gary had seen the charging mammoth, but Elara instinctively went the way Gary went.

Cherry Angel and Damien Blackwood, however, leapt aside to the right.

Everyone crashed down onto the forest grass.

The mammoth missed them all once more and rammed instead into the lopsided tent from which it had fished out its last victim. It became entangled in the tent, and began running about in circles while trying to get the tent off of its head.

Keeping a careful eye on the mammoth, Gary sat up. After noting that no one had been harmed by the mammoth's mad rush, he felt around for his cellphone, which he'd dropped in the confusion.

Gary also thought he heard a chopper overhead, a short distance away, but approaching them.

"Okay, guys," he said, while scanning the forest floor for his phone, "I just changed my mind. I think we'd better make a run for the parking lot while—" once again he froze.

Oh . . . God . . . NO!

A massive tree, which had been practically uprooted by the mammoth's violent charge and had been swaying precariously since then, now finally tipped over.

Gary watched helplessly as the tree crashed down on Cherry Angel and Damien Blackwood, who were both just getting up to their feet.

The falling tree knocked both of them back down to the ground. The noise it made while falling was as loud as one of the mammoth's rages.

Gary looked at the mammoth, which was still tangled up in the tent and was now circling round like a dog or a cat that was chasing its tail, then he leapt up and hurried over to the fallen tree.

He felt sick as he looked down at the two people pinned beneath it.

Damien Blackwood was already dead. His right arm and right leg were the only parts of his body visible outside of the giant trunk, and neither so much as twitched when Gary bent down and picked up the Weatherby rifle from his fingers.

Cherry Angel wasn't dead yet, but she soon would be. Just like with her dead boyfriend, most of her body was crushed under the fallen tree, but her right forearm and her head were out in the air. She was bleeding profusely from both her mouth and nostrils.

Cherry had an expectant look on her face as if she wanted some words of comfort from Gary. He wondered what he could say to her that would be of any help.

"Dying like this sucks, ranger," Cherry said and died.

Gary straightened up and frowned. Then he looked around for Elara.

Elara had fainted, either during or after the mammoth's attack. He watched her start to stir and then turned his attention to the cause of all this death.

The mammoth was still tangled up. Try as it might, it seemingly couldn't work its head free of the tent fabric. After each failed attempt to remove the tent, it roared angrily up at the sky. Its frustrated noises mingled with the sound of that helicopter that Gary had been hearing for a while now.

Gary smiled coldly at the mammoth. "Well, boy, I couldn't have asked for a better opportunity to kill you, or a more perfect range and angle."

He worked the bolt to chamber a fresh round and the chamber came up empty.

Gary stared at the gun in disbelief.

What the hell? I'm out of bullets?

He looked across at the tangled-up killer animal and wondered if he had the time to get over to the parking lot and retrieve the box of cartridges from his truck and then make it back here, before the mammoth was able to kill someone else.

I could shoot it with my pistol, but that won't do any good. I'll just enrage it further like I did before.

Elara was awake now, and was staring at her friends who were crushed under the tree, and like she'd soon faint again.

But then Gary heard voices approaching fast through the trees.

Is that the chopper crew I'm hearing?

But no, he could still hear the helicopter hovering somewhere nearby.

A moment later four men walked out of the woods next to Gary and Elara. One of them was an old guy, elderly, in his sixties or so. The other three were younger men. Two of them looked tough, like soldiers, and carried tranquilizer guns. The third man wore thick spectacles, and like their elderly leader, was clearly a scientist; he was carrying a transparent box of tranquilizer darts.

"Who are you guys?" Gary asked the four men.

"I'm Dr. Milton Ambrose the old scientist replied. "We're from the F-Bio research facility." Frowning, he pointed at the tangled up and frustrated mammoth. "Snuffy over there belongs to us, and we're here to take him back home where he belongs."

"Snuffy?" Elara asked. "That's its name?"

"You know, like the furry Muppet from Sesame Street," Dr. Milton Ambrose replied to her.

CHAPTER 41

"As you can see, your pet has been killing people," Gary told Dr. Milton Ambrose. "This is gonna cause a huge PR stink."

"Nothing that the US Government can't hush up," the younger scientist said coolly.

Gary looked inquiringly at Dr. Ambrose. "The government?"

"Yes, but let's put Snuffy to sleep first and I'll tell you more about it." Dr. Ambrose frowned, his confusion evident on his face. "What I don't understand is what turned Snuffy so violent all of a sudden. We saw the bodies at the car park when we arrived here, and now there are corpses everywhere here too. That's completely out of character for Snuffy."

"Normally, Snuffy wouldn't hurt a fly," the younger scientist explained. "He's as docile as a pet hamster."

"I can fill those details in for you," Gary said. "Just knock the damn mammoth out first."

Dr. Ambrose nodded and gestured to the two men with the tranquilizer guns. "Do it. Double dose."

"Just in time too," Gary said, on noticing that 'Snuffy' had just succeeded in ripping away the corner of tent that had been over his head.

As the woolly mammoth shouldered his way free of his encumbrance, both of the men with tranquilizer guns shouldered their weapons, took careful aim at the woolly mammoth, and fired.

The darts sailed through the air like missiles, and both scored direct hits.

"Double dose," Dr. Ambrose repeated in a calm voice. "We need to be sure he sleeps all the way back to his enclosure."

The younger scientist was already handing out fresh darts to the two men.

Both men loaded up their guns and fired again. Once again, both men scored direct hits on Snuffy.

Dr. Milton Ambrose nodded in satisfaction.

"In a few minutes, he'll be asleep," he told Gary.

CHAPTER 42

Just about to charge at the humans who'd gathered at the edge of the clearing, Snuffy felt the impact of the tranquilizer darts like gnats biting him, negligible pricks not worth considering.

As intended, the four darts' contents entered Snuffy's bloodstream and spread quickly through the woolly mammoth's body.

The problem was that the animal the tranquilizers had been intended for wasn't the animal they'd been injected into.

By now, the massive quantity of Agent Orange that Snuffy had consumed had altered his body so much that the tranquilizers were absorbed and metabolized in the same way that vitamins would be.

With the end result that the tranquilizers had no effect whatsoever on the killer mammoth.

CHAPTER 43

While waiting for Snuffy to fall asleep, Gary had been giving Dr. Ambrose a crash course in Agent Orange addiction as it applied to animals.

"Yes, I now understand what happened," the doctor said grimly. "We have a quantity of Agent Orange in our lab, which law enforcement wants analyzed so we can synthesize an antidote for its effects. And for ages I've been requesting that the narcotic not be kept in the same safe where we kept Snuffy's dietary supplements, but no one paid attention to my concerns. So, Paula must've gotten them mixed up when she was feeding Snuf—"

"I think we've a problem, doctor," the younger scientist interrupted.

"Huh?" Dr. Ambrose and Gary both paid proper attention to the mammoth again.

"The tranks don't seem to be working, sir," the young man said. "Snuffy should've been asleep two minutes ago."

Dr. Ambrose studied Snuffy's upright and alert pose and then checked his wristwatch. "You're right, Stanford. I wonder what is the matter?"

Snuffy began walking towards them, slowly but purposefully, his speed increasing perceptibly with each step.

"We'll up the dose then," Dr. Ambrose said, his voice a little nervous now. He gestured at the two men with the tranquilizer guns. "Once more, single dose this time."

The two men had reloaded during Gary's explanation. They aimed their guns again.

But then Gary said, "Hey, doc, that animal wasn't even fazed by what you hit it with the first time, and now it's heading right for us. I suggest we get the hell out of Dodge City, before we wind up like the rest of the corpses here."

"And I second that suggestion," Elara Nightshade said.

Without waiting for anyone's reply, Elara set off running towards the parking lot.

"I think she's too scared to remember she should put on some clothes first," Gary told Dr. Ambrose and his men. "Though you can see for yourselves that she never forgets her cell phone."

And then, seeing that Snuffy seemed about to break into a charge again, Gary hightailed it out of the clearing after Elara. For his own part, he had no idea where his cell phone had gotten to, and at the moment, he couldn't care less.

Gary's single glance back revealed that Dr. Ambrose and his three assistants weren't too far behind him. The four men were running for their lives, too, with Snuffy, the killer mammoth, hot on their heels.

CHAPTER 44

While running towards the parking lot, Gary heard the sound of the helicopter almost directly overhead now.

He looked up once, saw that that the chopper was headed in their direction and descending towards the trees, and then he kept on running.

The riddle of the helicopter was one to be solved later.

I guess it's heading for the campsite we're all running away from.

Wheezing for breath as he fled toward safety, Gary Bentley figured out his plan of action:

Okay, now that the doctor's planned intervention has failed, I need to get the bullets for this Weatherby out of my truck, load up again, and kill Snuffy the Mammoth. Damn! His name sounds like 'snuff', as in snuff movie, where real folks are killed in real life, folks killed for the entertainment of others!

So far, Snuffy hadn't killed anyone else, but Gary could clearly hear the animal crashing along behind them all, with Snuffy's progress only slightly impeded by the trees in his path.

The helicopter was now well behind them.

Propelled by her fright, Elara was still well ahead of Gary, while he, galvanized by his desire to kill Snuffy and end all of this madness, was in turn ahead off the doctor and his men.

And maybe, just maybe, because Dr. Ambrose's intention in all of this was to keep his prized reanimated animal alive, he and his crew were symbolically last in line.

Gary held on tight to the Weatherby rifle, gripping it like it was his most precious possession. He'd already lost his cell phone somewhere behind them. He knew he couldn't afford to drop the rifle, no matter what happened.

If I do that, we're all gonna be extinct as everyone but us thinks mammoths still are!

His breath wheezing from his lungs, Gary ran, ran, ran, until he could see the wide expanse of the parking lot appear between the trees.

CHAPTER 45

"Hey, that's it, down there!" Ray Linn called out to Brady as their helicopter cleared the campground parking lot and flew over the woods that bordered the river.

"Where?" Brady asked.

Ray began pointing. "Up ahead over there! I can see the mammoth. Shit, it's chasing a bunch of people into the trees!"

Brady aimed the helicopter in the direction she was indicating. After a while, he saw it too: the mammoth was charging after a group of people that included a naked woman. The woman was in front, a forest ranger was behind her, and then four more men were bringing up the rear.

"What do we do now?" he asked Ray. "Turn the chopper around and help them?"

Ray had their tranquilizer gun in her lap. "Not yet. First of all, I wanna see exactly where they're all coming from."

"Ray, baby, those people need our help," Brady objected.

She shook her head. "Not yet, they don't. There's still a good amount of space between them and the mammoth. It's not able to reach them because there's so many trees in the way. Take us on ahead, over to that clearing near the river, and then take us down low. I can't say for sure, but it looks like there was a major commotion over there."

Brady flew on forward until they were hovering over the destroyed campsite.

"Fuck! I can't believe what I'm seeing," Ray said as her eyes surveyed the carnage and the dead bodies everywhere. "This is fantastic!"

"I think I'm gonna be sick," Brady said. "What the hell do you mean this is fantastic? The clearing is full of dead people."

Ray grinned at him. "Don't you get it, baby? This entire mess is the fault of that asshole Dr. Ambrose and his creepy crew of scientists. I just knew something was wrong over there. And now I've the proof of it."

Brady looked sicker now than before. "Can we fly back now and see if we can help those people? They must've reached the parking lot by now. Out there, they won't have any cover from that monster. We may be able to airlift them to safety." He gestured out of the helicopter window down at the trampled corpses everywhere and then whistled in shock. "Shit, what the hell happened to that girl? Her head's up in a tree, and her body is down on the ground, and her neck is stretched thin as a jump rope."

Ray quickly unbuttoned her safety belt. "Hey, man, stop being such a damn wuss. Put the chopper down on the ground, but keep the engine running."

Brady gaped at her. "What the hell do you wanna do down there for?"

She waved her cell phone at him. "What else but to take pictures." She smiled coldly at Brady. "Those assholes at F-Bio have had this coming forever, and now, by letting this killer mammoth loose, they've dug their own graves and ordered their caskets to boot. No one will ever believe this without stone-cold evidence, so I'm gonna record as much evidence for the public as I can." She leaned over and kissed Brady on the cheek, too elated to notice that he tried to avoid the kiss. "And once I've filmed all of this death here, you and I can then fly back over to the parking lot and save the day." She grinned broadly. "We'll be heroes!"

"If you say so," Brady replied his male girlfriend. "I'd never have believed you were this coldhearted."

Ray said, "It's not my fault that the world is a toilet, honey. I'm just taking my own shit in it."

Brady nodded and put the helicopter down on the forest floor. "Okay, but hurry it up. Don't take forever like you're using the bathroom."

"I love you too, sweetie," Ray said, blowing him a kiss.

And then she climbed out of the helicopter, ran out beneath the whirling rotors, and began filming the dead people.

Oh, this is just fantastic, Ray thought as she gathered more and more morbid footage. *Milton Ambrose and his group of quacks won't stand a chance when I present this evidence of the results of their tampering with nature. They must've really been abusing that mammoth, testing all sort of chemicals on it and slowly driving it crazy.*

She walked over to the dead woman with the stretched-out neck and filmed her from head to toes. Then she walked over to film a man who'd died because the entire middle area of his torso had been stomped into the ground beneath the rest of his body.

Then Ray looked back over at Brady and the helicopter.

Brady had given in to his nausea and was busy retching out of the chopper window.

"Fucking hurry up," he called out miserably afterward. "I can't take much more of this. I feel like I'm in hell."

What a fucking wimp, Ray thought angrily. *I can't believe I ever slept with him. Oh, once I'm famous, I can do better, so much better. I can have any man I want then. But I'll only date the hot and woke ones, of course.*

She returned her attention to the corpses. *Oh, here's an interesting one, but where the hell is her head?*

Then Ray frowned:

I can't believe they were all calling me Ms. Pronouns behind my back. Well, assholes, we'll see who has the last laugh!

She pulled aside a stretch of tent canvas and delightedly filmed three or four people who'd been trampled into a gluey mess the coroners would find impossible to separate.

Behind her, Brady threw up again on seeing what she'd just uncovered.

Ray, however, was in vindictive heaven and ignored his misery.

"Hurry up, hurry up," Brady yelled at her over the noise of the chopper engines.

"Not yet, we've got to properly document what's happened here."

"But those people may be dying over there!"

"Shut up, asshole!" she screamed back at him. "Let them die! Their sacrifice will save lots of other lives!"

CHAPTER 46

Over at the parking lot, the situation was a dire one.

The fleeing group of six had split up in two once they'd reached the parking lot.

It had been a natural split: the group from F-Bio had all run off together towards their bus, while Elara had followed Gary over to his pickup truck.

But there was no time to even breathe before, having lucked onto the trail he'd forced through the trees on his way to the band's camping site, Snuffy, the Woolly Mammoth, charged out into the parking lot after them.

"Okay, get in the back and keep out of sight," Gary told Elara. "Don't worry, things will work out right."

Elara hid herself like he'd instructed, but she was so frightened by the mammoth's reappearance that, while lying down, she knocked the box of Weatherby cartridges off of the backseat and spilled them all under the front seat.

With time ticking away by the second, Gary ducked down in the rear foot well and began fishing the spilled cartridges out.

Gary Bentley was fortunate in that he'd parked first in line on that row of parking spaces.

Dr. Milton Ambrose and his crew were less fortunate, however. In their hurry to reach the woods, they'd parked their bus much closer to the tree line and because of this, once Snuffy emerged from the woods, he instinctively charged at them first.

The young scientist, Stanford, was about to open the bus when Snuffy charged at them. Stanford immediately panicked and dropped the bus's keys. Then, followed closely behind by Dr. Ambrose and the two security guards, he ran around to the other side of the bus.

Stanford could at least have opened the driver's door from this side, but he'd left the keys on the ground on the passenger's side of the bus where he'd dropped them. While everyone else cowered in fright and tried not to alert Snuffy to their presence behind the bus, one of the guards bit the bullet and ran around their vehicle to retrieve the key. He picked up the key, and then Snuffy gored him, and flipped him away through the air.

The sheer shock of seeing their companion flying like a shot bird momentarily paralyzed the other three men.

Before they could move, the woolly mammoth dug its immense tusks beneath the bus and flipped the vehicle over on top of them. Stanford and the second security guard were crushed beneath the upturned bus.

Dr. Ambrose, who'd been standing behind the two men, leapt away just in time to avoid being similarly flattened.

However, the doctor didn't escape unscathed. The flipped bus shattered his right arm. With blood squirting out behind him from the bodies of the two dead men, Dr. Ambrose set off at a slow jog for Gary Bentley's truck.

CHAPTER 47

Gary wasn't watching the massacre, which was happening parallel to his making sure Elara was safe and then picking up the spilled cartridges for the Weatherby.

He was very aware of Snuffy's presence nearby. He heard the animal roaring and trumpeting, heard the crash of metal on the floor, and the screams of dying and wounded men, but forced himself to concentrate on getting enough bullets to stop the killer animal.

"Help me!" he heard Dr. Ambrose scream, and heard the man's desperate footsteps running towards him.

He looked up then. Dr. Milton Ambrose was nearing the car with the cute teardrop camper/trailer hitched behind it. But close behind the fleeing man, with his eyes glowing like light bulbs, came the mammoth.

Gary had so far loaded up one cartridge into the Weatherby. He chambered the round, took fast aim at the massive approaching bulk, and fired.

Once again, he winged the creature, which shrieked in pain but didn't stop chasing the fleeing scientist.

Gary had no chance to reload the rifle before Snuffy, the Woolly Mammoth, reached Dr. Ambrose.

It was crazy what happened. Snuffy rammed Dr. Ambrose against the side of the teardrop trailer with so much force that the doctor's head separated from his body, sliced cleanly off of his shoulders by the top of the camper.

While the doctor's body gushed blood and slipped down to the ground, his severed head bounced sideways and out of sight.

The force of impact also shoved the teardrop camper right at Gary, who was forced to once again fling himself out of harm's way before the camper slammed into the side of his truck. The impact slammed the truck door shut and made Elara Nightshade start screaming in terror.

Gary had landed on the grass that bordered the parking lot. His left leg ached badly, but thankfully, it wasn't broken. He still had his rifle, having managed to hold on to it while jumping out of harm's way, when the mammoth had forced the camper against his truck. He'd spilled the ammo back into the truck again, though.

He sat up and watched a new crazy spectacle, a further unexpected twist in this deadly tale.

This is one of the craziest days of my fucking life! he thought as the mammoth began jerking his head back and forth, pulling and pushing the teardrop camper this way and that.

Gary at first thought that maybe the animal was working out a long-held grudge against the dead scientist and was trying to head-butt him to a pulp, but then he realized the truth:

The damn animal is stuck. Snuffy slammed himself against the teardrop camper with so much force that at least one of his tusks is now tightly jammed somewhere beneath or inside the camper.

This may be my big chance to kill it, Gary decided, staring at the gun in his hands. *But I need to load it up first.*

But this would be easier intended than done. In his attempts to free himself of the camper (presumably so that he could then kill both Gary and Elara) Snuffy was still slamming the half-vehicle against Gary's ranger truck, in the backseat of which, after some more terrified screaming, Elara Nightshade had fainted again.

The cartridges that Gary needed were all on the side of the truck that was being beaten with the camper. Gary was stuck, and started trying to figure out another way to get the ammunition, maybe by crawling over Elara.

With loud shrieks of rage, the mammoth dragged the trailer back and forth and jerked it up and down. Sparks filled the air as the camper scraped over the concrete flooring, and skid marks appeared as its tires were worn down by Snuffy's violence.

But he couldn't shake the camper free.

However, something unexpected did happen. All of a sudden, the hitch that linked the camper to the blue Nissan broke completely in two.

So, now the woolly mammoth was free, but he still had the camper stuck to his head.

And that was when the helicopter that Gary had earlier sighted flew down over the woods and headed for Snuffy.

Gary felt like heaving a sigh of relief. Some kind of help was arriving at last.

But what took them so long to return here? he wondered as the helicopter dropped lower and hovered over the parking lot.

CHAPTER 48

In the copilot's seat of the arriving helicopter, Ray Linn was now ready for action. Once more strapped in for safety, Ray had the loaded tranquilizer gun ready to fire.

"Okay, I got a bead on it. Keep the chopper steady."

"Looks like that camper vehicle is stuck on its head."

Ray nodded. "That makes the shot an easy one. Take me in a little closer."

Brady did so. "Hey, you're gonna need more than one trank to take down an animal that large." Then he groaned again.

"What is the matter *now?*" Ray asked him.

"The parking lot is full of corpses."

Ray nodded. "Look on the bright side, honey cakes. You and I are about to become national heroes."

"That's if we don't get crucified for killing the only mammoth in existence."

"We're not killing it. We're giving it some sleeping pills."

Ray took careful aim again. "Okay, keep 'er steady . . . and . . . Yeah, I got him."

She'd seen the dart bury itself deep in the mammoth's fur.

"Again, again. Hurry up!"

"Stop being nervous," Ray chided him as she reloaded the tranquilizer gun with a fresh dart. "The stupid animal can't even see us with that metal hat he's wearing."

But neither Ray Linn or her boyfriend had any idea what was about to happen.

CHAPTER 49

Down on the ground, Gary saw what the woman in the helicopter was trying to do.

He knew, however, that just like with Dr. Ambrose's futile attempt to sedate the mammoth, her efforts were doomed to failure.

But the helicopter, not the tranquilizers coming from it, was distracting Snuffy, who, with the camper still stuck to his tusks, was wheeling around to try and see what the noise above him was.

This was the opening that Gary needed. Once the mammoth was safely out of range, he hurried back to the side of his truck and forced open the door. Then he quickly picked up a handful of cartridges and began loading up the Weatherby Mark V.

Mindful of the danger if Snuffy the Mammoth turned his attention on him again, Gary kept an eye on the creature as he dragged his head left and right, while the woman in the copilot's seat of the helicopter continued peppering him with tranquilizer darts.

And that was how Gary clearly saw what happened.

All of this while, Snuffy had been fiercely trying to wrench the teardrop camper away from his tusks. And now, in a flash of brute strength, he finally succeeded.

The thing was, either intentionally or not, the mammoth flung the camper up into the air instead of sideways.

With his mouth open, Gary watched the teardrop camper detach from the woolly mammoth's head and fly up and collide with the hovering helicopter.

The inevitable happened. The airborne camper knocked the helicopter out of the air, a fall of about two hundred or so feet.

With the camper crash-landing further off, the helicopter (which the impact with the camper had knocked upside down, so that its rotors were now beneath it), crashed down ten yards or so away from Gary.

On the helicopter's impact with the concrete flooring, its top loudly imploded into its undercarriage, instantly crushing to death the couple seated inside of it. And then the helicopter caught fire, and a few seconds later, it exploded and burned like a furnace.

Shit, Gary thought as he watched burning pieces of metal fly off from the flaming wreckage. *I don't believe I just watched that happen.*

His attention was drawn back to his own problems by the mammoth's victorious roaring.

Gary turned towards Snuffy and discovered that the mammoth was already charging directly at him, with the clear intention of ramming him against the side of his pickup truck.

This time, however, with his gun properly loaded, he was ready for the rampaging beast.

CHAPTER 50

This was the moment of truth.

I miss this shot and I'm dead meat, Gary Bentley thought as the mammoth got closer and closer. He calmly noted that Snuffy's left tusk was broken in half.

That most likely happened when it flipped the teardrop camper up at the chopper.

Bizarrely, the huge animal was moving even faster than before, as if, instead of slowing him down, the tranquilizers that the woman in the helicopter had shot him with were some sort of performance-enhancing drug.

Gary Bentley sighted on Snuffy's head, drew a clear bead on his right eye, and fired.

At first, because the animal kept right on coming at him, he thought he'd missed this crucial shot like he had the ones in the woods.

But then, about five yards away from Gary, the killer mammoth's front legs buckled out from under him and he went down in a hairy heap.

Snuffy's body slid to a halt two yards from Gary. Gary saw the blood leaking from the hole he'd drilled into Snuffy's brain, near the inner corner of the mammoth's right eye, at the base of his trunk.

He relaxed. The nightmare was over. He looked around at the many dead bodies in the parking lot and at the burning helicopter. Then he peered down into rear of his truck, and saw Elara Nightshade staring back at him with relief in her eyes.

Time to call law enforcement, he thought. *And I need to find the girl some clothes before they turn up.*

CHAPTER 51

Calling from Elara Nightshade's cell phone, Gary finally got the guys at the ranger station to believe his story that a *woolly mammoth* had killed almost thirty people at the Sleepaway Campground.

Once he'd confirmed that help was on its way, he put away the Weatherby Mark V in the back of the truck, found Elara a blanket to wrap around herself, and waited.

Elara Nightshade was alive and well, but was shell-shocked after what she'd been through. Gary thought the young woman would be fine, though she might need some therapy to help her along the way.

Once Elara was wrapped up, she lay back down in the rear of the camper and went to sleep.

CHAPTER 52

Before law enforcement arrived at the campground, Gary had an unexpected meeting.

Gideon Thorne, Cherry Soufflé's video director, walked out of the woods, alive and well.

Gary stared at him in surprise. He'd forgotten all about Gideon.

Cleansed of mammoth dung now, the young man headed over to talk to Gary.

"Dammit, sir," he told Gary, "that was the craziest thing I ever saw in my damn life."

"You saw what happened?" he first inquired of him and then pointed down at the small video camera that Gideon was holding. "Don't tell me you filmed it all."

Gideon nodded grimly. "Yeah, I got most of it recorded. Not the massacre at the camp—thankfully, I missed that. But I got back to the camp from having my bath just as the mammoth was chasing you all out of there. So, I quickly pulled on some clean clothes, grabbed up a camera, and ran after you all, and then I recorded everything that happened here."

Gary stared at him. "Really?"

Gideon shrugged. "Well, first of all, I called the police, of course, but they didn't believe me, so . . ." The young man then shook his head in some disbelief. "When the mammoth flipped that camper up into the sky, Hollywood would've been proud. Sir, you'll make a great hero. That was some damn fine shooting, sir."

"What are you gonna do with the footage?" Gary asked. "I mean, you know the government won't let you keep it. It's too sensitive."

Gary then gestured at the dead animal that lay just a few yards away from both of them, his head in a pool of his own blood, his eyes orange as fruit. "According to Dr. Ambrose, this was the only woolly mammoth in existence, and I just shot the damn thing."

Gideon Thorne walked over to stand beside Snuffy's body and filmed himself replying to Gary.

"Oh, I already uploaded everything to the internet," he said. "Nothing gets lost there. The truth is always up on the internet somewhere."

The End

ABOUT THE AUTHOR

Gary Lee Vincent was born in Clarksburg, West Virginia, and is an accomplished author, musician, actor, producer, director, and entrepreneur. In 2010, his horror novel *Darkened Hills* was selected as 2010 Book of the Year winner by *Foreword Reviews Magazine* and became the pilot novel for *DARKENED - THE WEST VIRGINIA VAMPIRE SERIES*, which encompasses the novels *Darkened Hills, Darkened Hollows, Darkened Waters, Darkened Souls, Darkened Minds* and *Darkened Destinies*.

He has also authored the bizarro thriller *Passageway*, a tribute to H.P. Lovecraft, *When the Bedposts Shake*, an erotic horror, *THE BLACK CIRCLE CHRONICLES*, a five-part mini-series that includes the books *Prove Your Love, Strange New Powers, Night Wings, Sheep Amongst Wolves,* and *Lord of the Birds,* and the *CRACKIMALS* series of horror-comedies (featuring titles *Crackcoon, Crackodile, Cracksquatch, Crackroaches, Crackadillo, Crackaroo, and Crackmammoth*).

Gary co-authored the novel *Belly Timber* with John Russo, Solon Tsangaras, Dustin Kay, and Ken Wallace and *Attack of the Melonheads* with Bob Gray and Solon Tsangaras.

As an actor, Gary has appeared in over a hundred feature films, including *Prove Your Love, Faded Memories, Midnight,* and *My Uncle John is a Zombie,* and multiple television series, including *House of Cards, Mindhunter, The Walking Dead,* and *Stranger Things.* You can also find Gary in the motion picture adaptation of *Crackcoon* from Director Brad Twigg, playing Jonathan, the forest ranger.

Gary made his directorial debut with *A Promise to Astrid.* He has also directed the films *Desk Clerk, Dispatched, Midnight, Godsend, Strange Friends,* and *Shoulder Down: Road to Redemption.*

OTHER GREAT TITLES FROM

WWW.BURNINGBULBPUBLISHING.COM

"Lots of action!" — Kimberly Bennett
Author, *Twisted Delights*

GARY LEE VINCENT

PASSAGEWAY

"This is a book that will keep you intrigued to the very end!"
—Christine Soltis, Author *Final Moon*

GARY LEE VINCENT'S
DARKENED
THE WEST VIRGINIA VAMPIRE SERIES

DARKENED HILLS

When evil descends on a small West Virginia town, who will survive?

Jonathan did not start out his life to become a rambler, it justworked out that way. William was a troubled youth with something to hide. Both were from Melas, a small town tucked away in the West Virginia hills... a town where disappearances are happening more and more frequently.

After the suicide of a wanted serial killer, the townsfolk thought the nightmare was over. But when a centuries-old vampire is discovered they find out the hard way it's just getting started. Dark secrets can only stay hidden for so long and when the devil comes to collect, there will be hell to pay. Can Jonathan and William find a way to stop the vampire before it's too late? Find out in *Darkened Hills!*

DARKENED HOLLOWS

In the heart-stopping sequel to the award-winning *Darkened Hills*, Jonathan and William must return to West Virginia to face possible criminal charges stemming from their last visit to the damned town of Melas, where both had narrowly escaped the clutches of a vampire seethe.

And as livestock start mysteriously getting murdered with all of their blood drained, worried farmers are searching for answers - leaving the local Sheriff and his deputy racing against time to learn the cause before a more violent crime is committed.

WWW.DARKENEDHILLS.COM

GARY LEE VINCENT'S
DARKENED
THE WEST VIRGINIA VAMPIRE SERIES

DARKENED WATERS

When the world goes to hell, the chosen must arise!

As Talman Cane orchestrates a flood of epic proportions in this third installment of the *Darkened* series the towns of Melas and Tarklin are caught completely off guard by the deluge. Hell-bent on finishing what they started, the evil brothers return to the lunatic asylum to take care of the witnesses and add to the ever-growing army of the undead.

Aided by Lucifer himself and the insane vampire demon Legion, the stage is set to channel all of the forces of hell to come forth. In an all-out race to survive, Jonathan, William, and Amanda soon discover they are up against impossible odds as Lucifer opens the Gateway to Hell, ushering in the zombie apocalypse and the End Times.

Find out who will survive this cosmic battle of the ages in *Darkened Waters!*

DARKENED SOULS

Melas and the Madison House are about to be rebuilt.
True evil is about to be reborne!

Young ex-priest and vampire-killer William is drawn back to the West Virginian town that almost killed him, where his vampire arch-enemy Victor Rothenstein still stalks the earth.

The town of Melas lies destroyed after the battle of the End of Days. But why is wealthy Jackie Nixon so eager to rebuild it using the bone dust of murdered souls?

Terrible evil has visited before, but the Gateway to Hell is about to be reopened in a horrific climax. And this time – it's personal.

WWW.DARKENEDHILLS.COM

Burning Bulb

GARY LEE VINCENT'S
DARKENED
THE WEST VIRGINIA VAMPIRE SERIES

DARKENED MINDS

Jackie Nixon intends to become Vampire Queen, but at what blood-drenched cost?

In this continuation to the explosive infernal saga begun in Darkened Souls, newly-turned vampire Jackie Nixon is taking no prisoners. Accompanied by her daughter, Kate, and by the captive vampire lord Victor Rothenstein, Jackie Nixon explores the Darkness. There, she intends to rouse the slumbering vampire race, bound under an ancient curse, and with their help, rule the human world.

But there's a deadly threat to Jackie's plans. Not just William who is trying to stop her, but her own royal ambitions. If Jackie performs the ritual to wake the sleeping vampires the wrong way, she could instead free the Red Beast of Hell, an unspeakable evil that even the undead fear.

DARKENED DESTINIES

With over 45 people missing after Jackie Nixon's party, the mysteries surrounding Melas and the Madison House keep getting darker.

Now, with legions of vampires at her command, can anything or anyone stop her from gaining complete control over all mankind?

The final battle has begun! As the Vampire Queen ascends her throne and sets to unleash the full forces of darkness, the fate of all things good hangs in the balance.

Burning Bulb
PUBLISHING

WWW.DARKENEDHILLS.COM

WHEN THE BEDPOSTS SHAKE

An Erotic Terror

GARY LEE VINCENT

STRANGE
FRIENDS

GARY LEE VINCENT

PROVE YOUR LOVE

GARY LEE VINCENT

STRANGE NEW
POWERS

THE BLACK CIRCLE CHRONICLES - BOOK 2

GARY LEE VINCENT

NIGHT
WINGS

THE BLACK CIRCLE CHRONICLES - BOOK 3

GARY LEE VINCENT

SHEEP AMONGST
WOLVES

THE BLACK CIRCLE CHRONICLES – BOOK 4

GARY LEE VINCENT

LORD OF THE
BIRDS

THE BLACK CIRCLE CHRONICLES - BOOK 5

GARY LEE VINCENT

From the Creator of DARKENED HILLS...

RIVER
A VAMPIRE'S NIGHTMARE

GARY LEE VINCENT

A Vampire's Nightmare Continues . . .

RIVER

BOOK **2** ICARUS

GARY LEE VINCENT

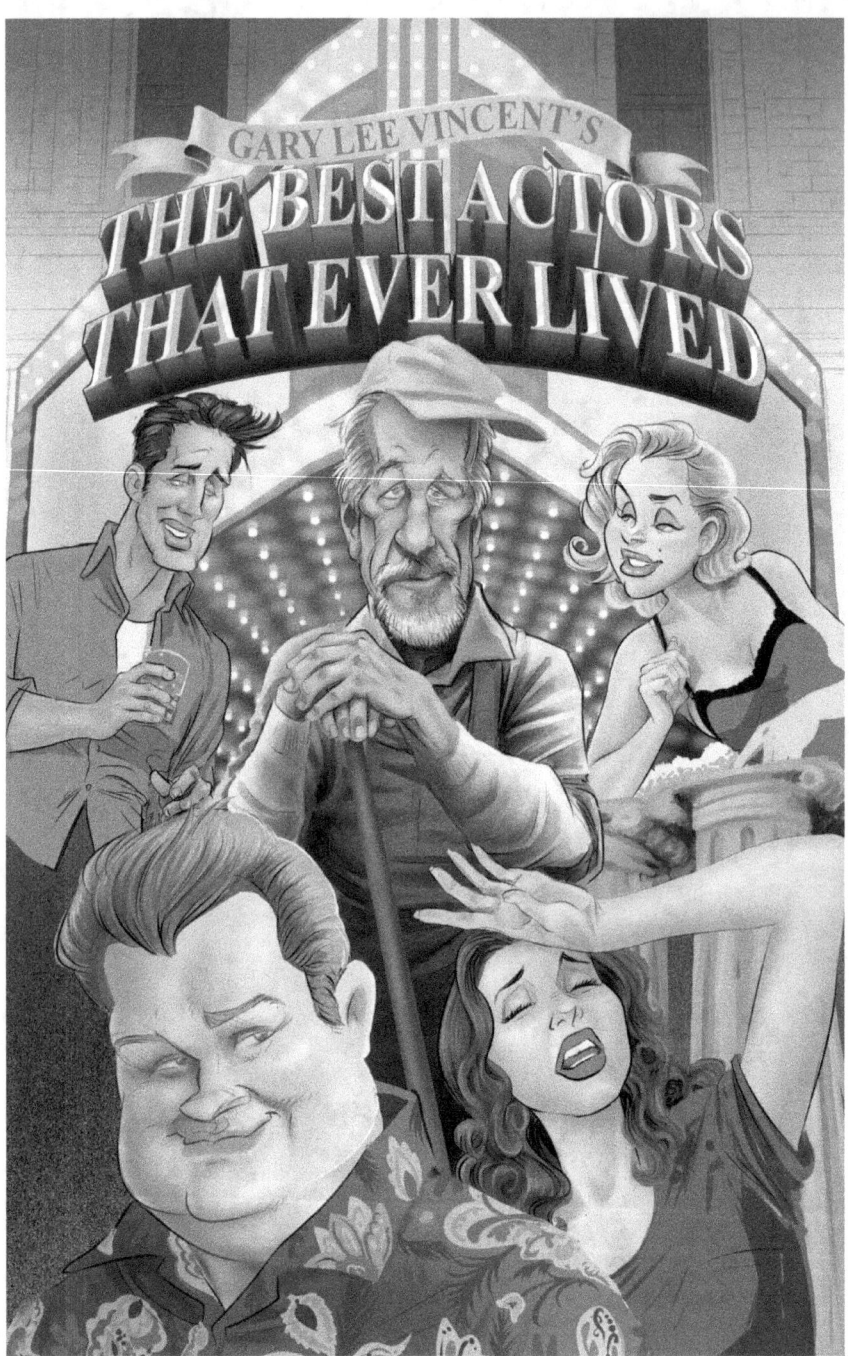

JEROME

A GHOST STORY

GARY LEE VINCENT

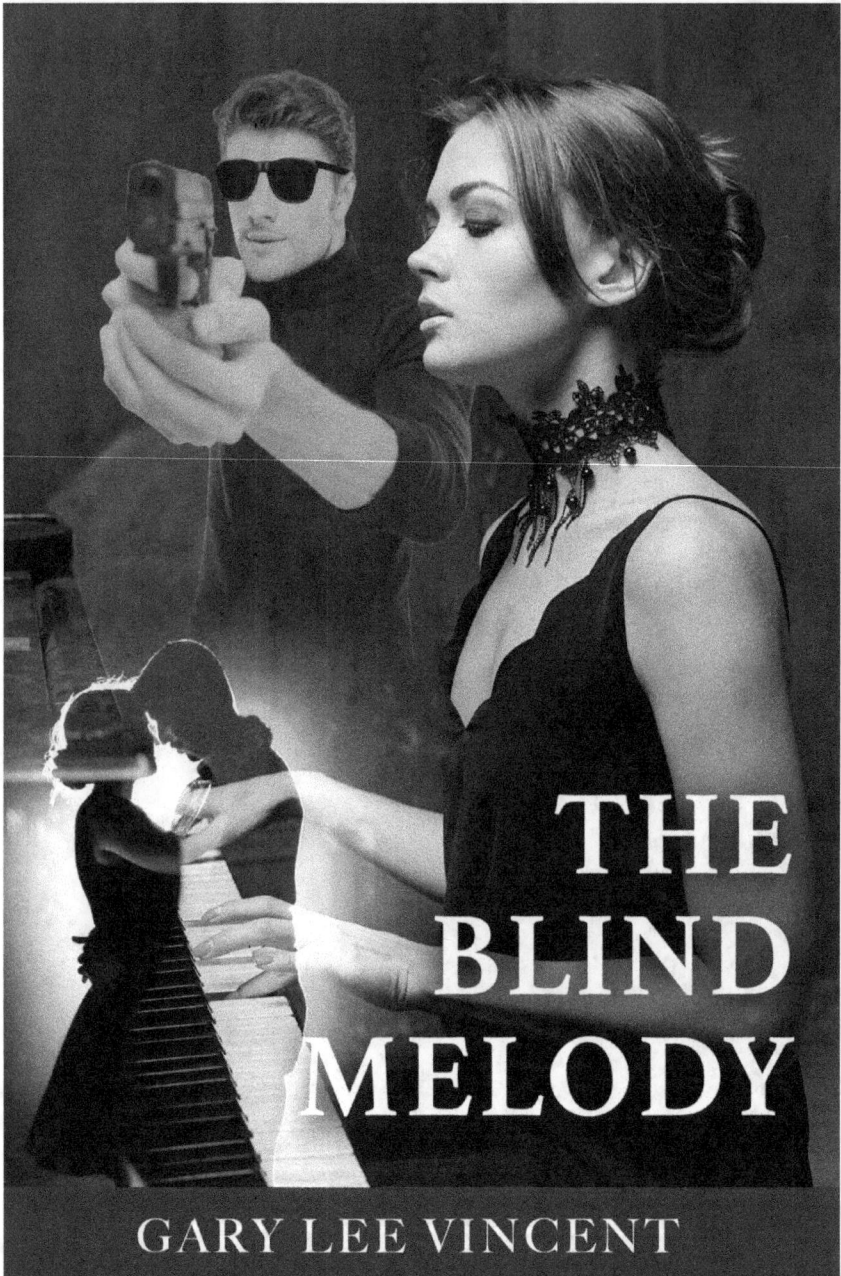

THE
BLIND
MELODY

GARY LEE VINCENT

RISE OF THE DEAD

AN EARTH-SHATTERING ANTHOLOGY OF ZOMBIE TERROR

Featuring Stories By:

John A. Russo   Tyson Blue   E.L. Slice   Nelson W. Pyles

Andy Rausch   Stephen Spignesi   R.D. Riley   Zakary McGaha

David J. Fairhead   Gary Lee Vincent   David C. Hayes   Rachel Montgomery

Paul Victor Wargelin   David F. Walker   William Vitka

Rich Bottles Jr.   Douglas Brode

www.ingramcontent.com/pod-product-compliance
Lightning Source LLC
Chambersburg PA
CBHW070935250626
47159CB00009B/3258